# Rainbow Dorm
# Diaries

# Rainbow Dorm Diaries

*The Yellow Dorm*

FARZEEN ASHIK

PARTRIDGE

ISBN:        Hardcover        978-1-5437-0010-7
             Softcover        978-1-5437-0009-1
             eBook            978-1-5437-0008-4

**To order additional copies of this book, contact**
Partridge India
000 800 10062 62
orders.india@partridgepublishing.com

www.partridgepublishing.com/india

# CONTENTS

# Chapter 1

May 1992

# ARTHI

The glorious orange-red blossoms of the gulmohar tree shone in the bright sunlight. It was a splendid May morning, and Arthi swung out of bed, grinning from ear to ear. Sunday was her favourite day of the week. That was the only day she was left to her own devices, which meant she could get up way after her normal wake-up time of 6 a.m. and do whatever she pleased, which normally meant curling up lazily in bed with a book or two after an enormous breakfast.

Her stomach rumbled at the thought of food and she quickly rushed through her morning ablutions. She took the steps two at a time and flung herself into the dining room, where the table was laden with all sorts of breakfast goodies. Her parents were not down yet and so she ran around the oval teak table, lifting the tops of the dishes to unearth their treasures. Her eyes glistened with delight as she took in the spread—crispy golden-brown masala dosa, light-as-a-feather idlis, a piping hot aromatic sambar, and three different coconut chutneys coloured green, white, and orange. Arthi was a foodie, and her mother often said the words *bottomless pit* were created for her.

Shanti Akka, their all-in-one *cook-cleaner-nanny*, made the best food in the whole world. She was a rotund, greying, ageless member of the house. She had been around since Arthi was an infant. Arthi skipped happily to the kitchen, her curly black hair bouncing as she went.

'Shanti Akkaaaaa! The breakfast looks amazing,' Arthi complimented her in Tamil.

Shanti Akka gave her a merry smile that lit up the entire kitchen. She loved Arthi dearly.

The sound of raised voices pierced the warmth and aroma of the kitchen. *They are fighting again! This is going to be one of those days*, thought Arthi, her smile slipping from her face. Shanti Akka quickly closed the kitchen door, hoping to keep the nasty arguments away from Arthi. But the voices got louder and angrier. Arthi stood rooted to the spot and listened to bits and pieces of the heated conversation that came through to the kitchen. She heard her name a couple of times and something about *school* and *discipline*. She winced at some of the ugly words that reached her ears, turning them pink.

Her parents were always fighting, at least as far back as she could remember. *Thank God they haven't thrown things at each other today*, she thought. The last fight had been an ugly one, and Shanti Akka was the one left picking up pieces of broken vases and porcelain plates while Arthi watched in horror.

'I think they've stopped now. Why don't you go in, ma, and eat your breakfast. I'll make you a fresh, hot masala dosa right away,' said Shanti Akka, gently prodding her towards the dining room.

Arthi nodded and carefully opened the kitchen door and quietly made her way to her place at the table. Both her parents were engrossed in their individual newspapers now. Her father read only Tamil papers and her mother only English. Her father peered out from behind his paper when her chair creaked.

'Arthi, what plans for the day?' he asked.

'Nothing, Appa.'

'Hmm . . . children these days don't have the focus we had during our day. Did you read today's paper?'

'No, Appa. I just woke up and came down.'

Her father snorted and muttered something unflattering about her reading habits and lack of interest in current affairs and buried himself in the paper again.

Arthi exhaled in relief, she hadn't even realized she was holding her breath in the first place. Her interactions with her father always ended the same way, with a snort of disapproval or disappointment or disgust. He had always wanted a son but the gods had thought otherwise.

She looked over to the other side of the table and saw her mother smiling at her. People said she was a carbon copy of her mother: with skin the colour of strong, filter coffee, lively black eyes, and wild, curly hair. They were poles apart from her father, who was tall, fair, and very Aryan. He was a typical Tam-Bram, handsome and brilliant but with a vicious tongue.

Shanti Akka bustled in with a golden masala dosa that stood out like the wing of a Boeing 737, and Arthi was grateful for the diversion. The only sound in the dining room was of delicious food being put away into eager stomachs and the occasional sound of cutlery. To Arthi, *this* was what peace sounded like.

Arthi's parents argued about everything under the sun: politics, family, work, holiday destinations, friendships, money! She wondered *why* they got married and *why* they still stayed together if they didn't get along. Her cousins from US had told her that people there got a 'divorce' if they were unhappy with each other. And to Arthi her parents seemed to fit the bill for getting this thing. They were *definitely* unhappy and *especially* unpleasant around each other.

With breakfast out of the way, each member of the family made their way into their individual comfort zones in the house, as far away from each other as possible. An uneasy truce reigned and no one wanted to rock the boat. Arthi crept back into bed with her latest book, *Anne of Green Gables*. She had just reached the third chapter when she heard a knock and her mother's curls popped in.

'Arthi, *kanna*, I need to talk to you about something,' she said.

'Sure, Amma,' Arthi replied, putting down her book.

Arthi loved her mother to bits (except when she was yelling at her Appa). She wanted to be just like her—smart, intelligent, always laughing, and full of fun. All her friends liked her mum; she threw the best birthday parties in town and never nagged her like the other mothers. Her friends envied their easy, open relationship.

'*Kanna*, remember I told you about this school in Ooty where some of my cousins studied years ago?'

Arthi nodded slowly, not sure where this was going.

'It's called the Royal Academy for Young Women and it's over a hundred years old. It's a fantastic boarding school and it would be perfect for you.'

Her mother's words came out in a rush, all together. Arthi felt like she was hit by a tsunami. *What? No Amma, no Shanti Akka, no Tessy (her best friend), and no old school.* It sounded like a recipe for disaster.

'Perfect for whom? Definitely not me!' she thought instantly.

Before she could open her mouth to protest, her mother continued.

'Your appa and I are having some problems and we are trying to work things out. But it's not an easy time for us. I don't want you around while all this is happening. It's not good for a young girl to hear these kinds of unpleasant things; it poisons your mind. And I know you can't pick sides, we are both your parents and I want to keep things cordial so you can have your father as well.'

*What the heck is going on? Are they breaking up or staying together? What unpleasantness? I am already used to it, they don't have to send me away to protect me,* Arthi thought silently.

'Amma, I don't get it,' she said, shaking her head in confusion, like she was submerged underwater and couldn't hear her mother clearly.

'*Kanna*, we are getting a divorce,' her mother blurted out.

'Oh!' gasped Arthi. The pieces were falling into place now.

'We have tried to work things out for the past twelve years, and I'm sure you've noticed it's not been easy. Your father and I are *fundamentally* very different people. Unfortunately when our parents *arranged* our marriage, they thought we would adjust and get along,' she explained.

'But, Amma, why do you have to send *me* away then? Why can't I be here with you?' Arthi asked, tears rolling down her face.

The enormity of what was happening was slowly sinking in. Her shoulders seemed weighed down by some invisible burden and she was finding it hard to breathe, like someone had placed a really heavy flowerpot on her chest. She could see her mother crying through the veil of her own tears. She wanted to hug her but she couldn't; she was frozen.

'I'm sending you away because things will get messy. And neither I nor Appa want to hurt you,' she said softly.

Arthi looked out of her window and suddenly the world seemed grey and bleak in spite of all that sunshine.

NOORIE

The mango trees in the front yard stood like silent sentries waiting for the messenger of doom. Noorie had been on the lookout for the postman all week but was disappointed yet again. She had been waiting to intercept her report card before it fell into her father's hands. He was always bugging her about her maths marks that were never good enough for him.

Noorie had always been a mummy's girl. From the time she could crawl, she could be seen following her mother everywhere. And now, twelve years down the line, nothing had changed. Her father was irritated beyond measure and blamed her mother for her over-dependence and clinginess. Noorie couldn't understand what the fuss was all about. It was *her* mother after all. Weren't you supposed to be close to your mother? Wasn't that how things worked? But obviously her father (who called the shots in their house) thought differently.

Noorie shrugged away her worries and went back to the video game she had been playing with her best friend Vidya. The girls were enjoying Noorie's new video game, jumping over obstacles, climbing mountains, and shooting at their enemies on screen, shouting and whooping in delight as they crushed them and moved to the next level. They were nearly identical in appearance and inseparable since kindergarten. With heads of shiny, sleek black hair and mischievous smiles, the girls went arm in arm everywhere.

'Noorie! Come down, please!' yelled her father from below.

Noorie rolled her eyes at Vidya and went down reluctantly. Nobody messed with Noorie's father. He had a violent temper on a very short leash. The girls came down to the living room to find Noorie's parents and grandmother waiting for them. Her father was pacing the room like a caged lion. He plunged into the matter right away.

'So, your mother and I have decided that it's *high* time we make some changes in this house,' he paused, looking at Noorie, who was quelled under his gaze.

*What was happening? What had she done now? Did her report card have the dreaded red marks in them? How badly had she done in maths?* she thought as her shoulders slumped.

'We have decided to send you to a boarding school in Ooty. You will start class 7 on June 1st, when the school reopens,' he announced.

For a moment Noorie didn't react. She had been worrying about her report card and here was a bolt out of the blue. *Boarding school? What the heck was Papa talking about?*

'So?' he asked impatiently, irritated about not getting a reaction from his daughter.

'But . . . but . . . why?' she stammered, bug-eyed with shock.

'It's *time*, that why,' said Papa.

'Time for what?' she asked. She looked in bewilderment at her frozen mother.

'It's time to be *independent*. To do things for yourself, to be your own person, to forge your own identity,' continued her father. 'You get everything done for you here. Either your mother or grandmother or the maid does it for you. I don't want my daughter to grow up like *this*, into a useless, no-good person. I want you to make *something* of yourself.'

*'But I'm only twelve years old! What do you expect me to make myself into?'* she screamed in her head but she didn't dare question her father aloud.

'Royal Academy for Young Women is a great school known for creating leaders and that's what I want you to become, *a leader*. You better not disappoint me, child. I hope you have at least *some* of my genes,' he concluded, throwing a glance of contempt at her silent mother.

Noorie found herself sitting down on one of the sofas, dazed and confused. No one was saying anything. Her father had left the room. He had no patience for females and their emotions.

'Mummy . . .' she began.

'He wants only the best for you, Noorie,' replied her mother softly.

Noorie felt as though someone had stabbed her in her chest, the pain was so intense. Even her mother seemed to have forsaken her.

*Am I so disappointing? Why have they all abandoned me? Have I done something terrible? Why doesn't Mummy speak up for me? Why can't she stand up to him? Why is she so afraid all the time?*

And for the first time in her life, Noorie was angry with her saintlike mother.

'You are not going to do anything, are you?' she whispered.

Her anger pulsed in the room like an animal. Her mother tried to reason with her, to soften the blow somehow, but Noorie was beyond mollifying.

Vidya took her up to the room and the two girls sat silently on the bed. Noorie was not crying any more, she just looked out of the window mutinously.

'I'll make a mess of things,' said Noorie. 'I'll make them wish they never sent me there.'

Vidya had never seen her friend like this before. Noorie had always been a sweet girl who played by the rules. She never courted trouble and was keen to stay out of problems.

'Maybe it won't be so bad,' whispered Vidya.

Noorie silenced her with a steely look. She cursed her luck. Her mother would be no help and neither would her grandmother. Pleading with her father was out of question. She was too scared. She literally had no choice. She would have to go to this *stupid* school and that too in just three weeks.

## ROYAL ACADEMY FOR WOMEN, OOTY

May was a busy month for an otherwise sleepy town like Ooty. Set in the heart of the Nilgiris (which literally translated to Blue Mountains), Ooty was the crown jewel. Established decades ago by the British as a summer resort, the town was known for its beautiful man-made lake, the impeccably maintained botanical gardens, the race-course, the golf courses, and of course the prestigious boarding schools that graced its slopes.

And if Ooty was the queen of the Blue Mountains, then the *Royal Academy for Women* was a prized gem in her crown. The boarding school was established and run by a formidable group of nuns who had arrived in Ooty as missionaries. With over one hundred years of educational experience under their belt, the sisters of the Royal Academy of Women knew a thing or two about refining young girls and grooming them into leaders and visionaries of the future. The management, teachers, and students of this school set a bar so high that even after a century none of the other schools that cropped up in the hill station could match it. The academic elite wanted to teach there. And the cream of society wanted to learn there.

The school campus was abuzz with activity that hot May morning but not with young girls (as it usually was the case) but with dozens of workers—painters, carpenters, plumbers, masons, gardeners, and electricians. The men worked in groups at a frenzied pace, not because they were behind schedule but because two pairs of eyes watched them like hawks from either ends of the long horseshoe-shaped corridor. These women ruled this school with iron fists. From afar they looked like twins, attired in long crisp white tunics reaching just below their calves with long sleeves and high necks. A white coif extended like a bar from ear to ear, high on their foreheads and a long black veil covered their hair.

There were just two weeks left for school to reopen and the nuns were busy making sure that all repairs were being done and the school would be as good as new for the girls. The buildings glowed in the warm sunshine. A few workers were on the roof, replacing some of the broken red tiles; some of them were painting the ivory-coloured walls and removing any memory of a blemish. Carpenters worked on doors that needed oiling and fixing the glass on a few broken windowpanes.

The two middle-aged women met somewhere in the middle of the horseshoe, acknowledging each other with a nod. Both Sr. Josephine and Sr. Rosemary didn't see eye to eye on many things but being tough on the girls was one thing they agreed on unconditionally. They walked together from room to room, inspecting the walls, ceilings, electrical fixtures, and furniture to ensure that everything was in order. The two perfectionists were tough customers and the local workers dreaded their quick tempers.

'Last year's class 10 results were quite good, weren't they?' asked Sr. Josephine.

Sr. Rosemary snorted in disgust before saying, 'They could have been better. I kept telling Ms Amina to push them harder but no! She felt the girls were doing quite all right. And now look what happened, not a single one above 95 per cent.'

Sr. Josephine held her tongue. She knew how much the class 10 board exam results meant for Sr. Rosemary, who was an exemplary academician herself. In her opinion, the girls had done quite well indeed. The entire batch of thirty-five had scored above 80 per cent and a few had reached 90–92 per cent but the Nilgiris district topper had been from the *James Lawrence School* for the first time, and Sr. Rosemary had worked herself up into a rage.

The nuns continued doing their rounds in silence. They inspected the wooden floors that were sparkling after a good polish. The kitchens were being turned upside down as the pest control team worked zealously. They walked down to the courtyard and watched the men shaping the emerald-green hedges. Even the magnificent trees that stood on either side of the boulevard leading to the school were not spared. Men climbed the fir, pine, spruce, and eucalyptus trees, trimming and pruning the branches. The enormous iron gate was being repainted with steel-grey paint that made it seem even more menacing. Security guards in smart blue-and-white uniforms stood beside the painters inspecting their work.

The nuns ticked off the items on their list—

- Courtyard
- Boulevard and main gate
- Skating rink
- Sports ground
- Basketball courts
- Tennis courts
- Mini golf course
- Science and mathematics block
- Art, music, and literature block
- Multipurpose block
- Classrooms
- Dormitories
- Dining hall and kitchen
- Study hall
- Playrooms
- Wellness centre
- Library
- Assembly hall.

The nuns took almost a week to inspect every nook and corner of the school. Set in twenty acres of lush green gentle slopes, the school had grown over the decades, adding more and more blocks and courts to cater to the ever-increasing needs of its exclusive students. It was therefore no wonder that they received applications from across all the states of India and even from overseas. Children of professionals, politicians, civil servants, authors, musicians, diplomats, and even royalty rubbed shoulders with each other under the high-beamed ceilings of this prestigious school. To be accepted at the *Royal Academy for Women* was a prestige, a privilege not given to all, and the nuns had every intention of making sure their girls would be given the best and would be *moulded* into the finest young women in the nation.

# Chapter 2

# GET, SET, GO!

Arthi's room looked like a tornado had hit it. There were three open suitcases of varying sizes filled with clothes, shoes, boots, sweaters, blazers, mufflers, socks and so on. Three very heavy grey blankets lay folded at the foot of her bed. The air conditioning was working overtime to suppress the heat of a Madrasi summer but to no avail. She and her mother were sweating profusely and looked exhausted. The last two weeks had been so busy that Arthi barely had time to wrap her head around the monumental decision her parents had made. She was so busy worrying about the details of her school and the long list of things they had to bring that she didn't have time to pause and think about her parents' relationship.

Her father had left on a business trip with just a nod. Arthi was happy that the rest of her summer holidays wouldn't have angry voices and nasty arguments. Her mother and she pored over the extensive list and shopped maniacally. With just a week left for school to start, they were in pretty good shape in terms of preparation.

They had gone for a long walk on Marina beach after the announcement two weeks ago. Her mother had explained that in all likelihood, her parents would be living separately when she came back after her school term. She had mixed emotions. One part of her wanted them to iron out their differences and live together as a happy family, like her other friends. But another part of her wanted them to just break up and live peacefully *without* each other. She couldn't bear the fighting. It was ugly and hurtful, and she often heard too much for comfort. She knew her mother was strong; she had never seen her cry when she fought with her father but she felt she must be hurting inside somewhere.

Arthi wasn't too happy about leaving her old school and friends and starting all over in a new place. She wanted to protest and try to stick to her guns and stay back in Madras but she didn't have the heart to argue with her mother. *She has enough to deal with as it is, without me adding more*, she thought sadly. And so she had promised herself that she would do her utmost to make things work as smoothly as possible. She would give her mother whatever support she needed and would make as little trouble as possible. If things worked out as her mother expected them to, then she would be left with just one parent at the end of the year, and she didn't want to mess that up as well.

Arthi was angry with her father. They had always shared an uneasy, reluctant relationship. He always seemed to look down upon her and her mother, like he was superior to them in some secret way. In her eyes, her mother was just as qualified and intelligent as he was, and she was definitely more fun to be with. He was a snob and she didn't like him much, especially when he made nasty remarks about her friends. So she wasn't really *that* upset about the way things were turning out.

'We will leave for Ooty on Saturday morning, Arthi. That will give us enough time to settle ourselves and sightsee a bit as well. I have to drop you off to school by Sunday afternoon and you start classes on Monday morning,' said her mother.

Arthi nodded as she arranged things in her suitcase. *The Royal Academy for Young Women* sounded a little stuffy, and as it was a convent school, she was sure it would be strict. Her older cousins studied in a similar school in Delhi, and they said the nuns were very firm and their punishments severe. Arthi shuddered a little as she thought about it.

NOORIE

'The welcome kit from your new school is here, sweetie,' said her mother that morning at the breakfast table.

Noorie looked up with dull eyes from her plate of hot puris. She mumbled something and went back to eating with exaggerated concentration.

'Let's see what we have here,' continued her mother in a bright voice.

Noorie refused to answer her mother and continued chomping loudly, hoping her mother would just stop talking. Her father joined in as he sipped his hot chai.

'What's in the kit?' he boomed.

'Well, there is a booklet with details about the school and its history and everything,' said her mother.

She passed it on to her husband to have a look and he flipped through the pages hemming and hawing with interest.

'Very fancy indeed,' he pronounced. 'And a history of 125 years! Fantastic! And look at the architecture of the place. Very colonial, very British, don't you think?'

'My! Look at this rule book. It's as thick as a Bible!' exclaimed her mother in surprise.

Her father thumbed through the thick, black, leather-bound book with glossy pages. 'All children are expected to walk softy over the wooden stairs and will be punished severely if found stomping or running loudly. We expect that young ladies *must be seen and not heard*.' Her father looked pointedly at his daughter.

Noorie jumped up and went beside her father. The print from the book seemed to leap out of the page already admonishing Noorie for her sullen behaviour. She half-expected a nun to pop out and start spouting rules from that fat black book.

'*Children are not allowed to speak in raised voices while having meals in the dining room.* Interesting rules, no? I think you will find this an easy one since you are already practicing silence with us,' mocked her father. Noorie's expression became dark and stormy.

She listened angrily as her parents continued to read out more absurd rules from that insane book. They were smiling and nodding at each other. She couldn't see the fun in all this. All she could see was a bleak future in the hands of these nuns who made and executed these illogical rules.

*It sounded like prison. A penguin prison, with nuns running about in black and white! How am I going to get out of this? And the rules sound so scary,* she thought.

She decided to make things as hard as possible for her parents. Noorie refused to help her mother shop or pack. She wanted no part of it.

'If you don't see where I'm keeping it, then how will you know where to look?' said her mother in mounting despair.

She knew her daughter had a stubborn streak beneath her meek demeanour. For the past two weeks, Noorie had been surly and rude. She kept to her room most of the time and came out only for meals, which were eaten in heavy silence. Her father ignored her now-permanent sulky expression while her mother tried to cheer her up but in vain. She hoped fervently that Noorie's anger would recede by the time they reached school.

# Chapter 3

# STARTING OFF

Arthi looked at the school campus in awe. The pictures in the welcome kit didn't do it justice. The buildings seemed to tower over her. The facts she had read popped into her mind as she ran her eyes over the immaculate grounds of her new home. The school complex was over 125 years old and had been designed by a world-renowned architect. The tall ivory-coloured buildings with shining red roofs were arranged in a horseshoe-shaped layout and faced a large courtyard which was fast filling in with cars of many kinds and hues. The buildings were about six to seven feet above ground level, on a raised foundation, and this made them seem like skyscrapers.

Arthi could see many children walking around on the wide, covered corridor that ran along the entire perimeter of the horseshoe. There were three wide flights of grey stone stairs set at the centre, left, and right of the horseshoe. As she climbed the one in the centre, Arthi felt as though she was climbing onto a massive stage and a show was just about to begin.

Noorie stood with her parents in the queue of people in front of an enormous and intricately carved teak door.

'Sr. Josephine James—Boarding Mistress'—the overlarge black lettering popped out aggressively. The crowd in front of the office was buzzing with conversation. Noorie noticed that everyone was smartly dressed. The men were in formal suits or casual jackets and the ladies were fashionably dressed in ethnic Indian wear that looked very trendy and stylish even to a novice like her. The children wore dresses and skirts of styles Noorie had never seen before. She tugged shyly at her simple white cotton frock and her light pink sweater, suddenly conscious.

'Thank God we changed at the hotel,' whispered her mother, dazzled by the shimmering sari of the lady in front of her.

Her father just snorted into his grey coat in reply. The family in front of them had just finished their meeting and now it was their turn. Noorie took a deep breath as she entered the cavernous room of the boarding mistress. The sunlight streamed in through the enormous French windows giving the room a yellow glow. A magnificent, ivory-coloured pinewood cross was hung on one of the walls. Paintings of Jesus Christ, Mother Mary, and a few other Christian saints whom Noorie didn't recognize looked down upon them benevolently as they sat down in front of the largest desk she had ever seen. The woman behind it was just as impressive.

Though large, her movements were quick and precise. She had a fleshy face with sharp black eyes that looked like they could see into your soul. Noorie gulped in mounting panic.

'So, child, are you ready to start the most amazing journey of your life?' asked Sr. Josephine, piercing her with her stare.

She squirmed in her seat and tried to nod.

'The Royal Academy for Women is the school of leaders and winners. We will teach you to be just and principled, to be wise and ethical, and to serve our great nation with pride. Almost all of you enter the school as *ordinary* children. Our aim here is to make the ordinary *extra*ordinary. We will make you into diamonds but the journey will not be an easy one. Our standards are high and we have no room for failure. We embrace passion and perseverance and we reward results. Remember that, child. You have taken the first step to becoming extraordinary.' She paused and then continued. 'Now go on to the Yellow Dorm and have a word with Annie Nanny, she will sort things out for you and answer any questions you have. Parents, you have no need to worry. Your child is in good hands. You may write to me or call if you have any concerns. Thank you for your time.' So saying, the efficient boarding mistress dismissed Noorie and her family and waited to meet the next lot of parents.

'That was a very impressive nun,' muttered her father in awe, and he was a man not easily floored.

Noorie's head was still buzzing from all that *extraordinary* talk. What had her parents gotten her into? She felt a little out of place; she was sure she didn't have a single extraordinary bone in her body.

She wondered if she would ever fit in. All around her, people looked so much more confident and in control of their destinies than she did.

The Yellow Dorm was just as its name suggested. The walls were a pale lemon yellow, as were the curtains and the painted cupboards and eiderdowns on the bed. It was like walking into the warm heart of a pale sun. Annie Nanny was a wizened old woman whose age could not be guessed. She bustled with great energy from bed to bed, shouting orders and taking notes on a clipboard. Noorie's eyes fell upon the rows of identical beds laid out in the large hall and suddenly her heart clenched in fear. She would be spending the night here, in this room, with all these strange children, away from her parents for the first time in her life. Anger took a back seat and Grief took the wheel. She couldn't believe it was finally happening.

Her mother spoke to Annie Nanny, who guided them to her assigned bed. She watched, frozen, as they unpacked her suitcases. She numbly helped her mother lay out the blankets and make her bed like the other children. Her father was speaking to some parents a little away from them. Noorie's surly expression had disappeared and she was just a frightened little girl suddenly.

'Mummy,' she whispered once the unpacking was all done, 'I'm scared.'

Her mother gathered her in her arms and kissed the top of her head. Noorie inhaled her mother's scent as she buried her face in her shawl.

'It will all be OK after a few days, sweetie. I know it's terribly scary to be alone in a new place but this will be fantastic opportunity to make new friends. And in no time, you will adjust and be happy again,' she reassured her daughter.

'What if . . . what if . . . no one likes me?' she whispered, looking up at her mother in horror.

'Rubbish! You are a sweet child. You make friends quite easily, don't you? Just don't sulk and pout, OK?' said her mother with a wink.

'I'm sorry about that, Mummy,' sniffed Noorie.

That earned a little squeeze and kiss, and soon after, Noorie was pulled into her father's bear hug.

'Now, you be a good girl and make me proud, all right? Don't get into too much trouble!' boomed her father.

Noorie nodded, her eyes bright with unshed tears. She suddenly regretted being nasty to her parents during the last few weeks. She would only see them in December now and it seemed so far away.

Annie Nanny came over just then and took control of the situation.

'Noorie, come here, child. I need your help,' she said briskly while nodding at her parents to take their leave.

Her mother hesitated for a moment, then gave her a little smile and wave and walked to the door followed by her father. Noorie watched in mounting panic as they left. Annie Nanny was saying something, but it didn't seem to register in her brain. All she could hear was the loud thumping of her heart beating very, very fast while around her, everyone seemed to move in slow motion.

'Run! Run!' yelled her brain. 'Go and catch them before they leave!'

Noorie didn't hesitate; she bolted for the door. Once outside, she made her way through the crowds impatiently and tried to remember where her car was parked. There were so many vehicles in the courtyard now and she wasn't too sure. And then she saw her mother's orange shawl, just as she was getting into their car. She gave a loud sob and ran down the stone steps as fast as her legs could carry her, knocking down suitcases and children on her way down, oblivious to everyone and everything. And just as she reached the bottom of the stairs, the car gave a roar and left poor Noorie behind in a puff of exhaust fumes. She sat down shocked. She was alone for the first time in her life.

Noorie recovered after some time, made her way back to the Yellow Dorm. The whole school was filling up. She saw children laughing and talking, catching up with old friends and making new ones. She envied their ease and comfort and wished she could turn back time and be in Calicut again.

Annie Nanny gave her a stern look when she got back and she meekly made her way to her bed and sat down quietly. A mass of curls suddenly popped up from the side of the next bed, giving Noorie a start.

'Hi there! I think my Vaseline jar rolled under your bed. Can you pass it over, please?' asked a smiling face.

Noorie nodded and dived down in search of the missing jar.

'I'm Arthi and I'm new,' said the girl as she took the jar from Noorie.

'I'm new too,' replied Noorie, a tremble in her voice.

Her eyes threatened to well up with tears again so she quickly looked down and pretended to arrange something inside her footlocker. Arthi didn't say anything. She was sensitive enough to know that her neighbour was upset and needed some quiet time. Her mother came back after a chat with Annie Nanny and quickly helped her set up her locker and cupboard. Arthi was doing her best to be strong, just like her mother would expect her to be. Her mother would be leaving in a few minutes and then she would be on her own in this new place.

'*I mustn't upset her, I mustn't!*' thought Arthi fiercely, as her heart began to clench. She knew her mother would be just as lonely as her, and with things the way they were at home, she had no one to support her either. Her mother had explained to her that her grandparents didn't support the divorce. They had been horrified at the embarrassment it would cause in their social circles. Arthi had been shocked to realize that her angelic Thatha and Patti had come down very hard on her mother for her tough decision. Since then, every step of the way, she had wanted to make it easier for her mother. Somehow she felt more protective of her now.

Arthi and her mother held each other briefly and bid adieu with little drama. They mirrored one another's actions and emotions, like peas in a pod. Noorie watched them under heavy-lidded eyes and felt a little embarrassed by her earlier outburst. The girls sat quietly for a moment, lost in their own private little worlds, worrying about new friendships and missing old ones terribly.

A loud peal of bells broke their line of thought and jolted them back to the present.

'What do you think that's for?' asked Arthi.

'No idea.' Noorie shrugged.

'It's teatime, girls!' announced a girl with a wide smile and melting brown eyes. 'Come on! I'll take you to the dining room.'

Jenna was the Good Samaritan of the class, ever ready to lend a helping hand.

The girls introduced themselves and followed a bouncing Jenna up a flight of wooden stairs to an enormous dining hall. It was divided into three distinct areas painted pink, green, and blue for the little ones, juniors, and seniors respectively, explained Jenna. The girls would be assigned tables later during the week but for now could take any place in the green hall. Arthi and Noorie took in the rows and rows of dining tables that lay before them. Each table seated six and they were fast filling up. They quickly took their places near Jenna and looked at the food that lay piled high at the centre of each table.

Fragrant brown loaves of fresh bread, golden-yellow butter balls, and a jar of school-made strawberry jam welcomed them. Both Arthi and Noorie realized they were ravenous and they tucked in happily. Three more girls rushed to their table, talking among themselves. Jenna introduced them as Radhica, Savita, and Zeenath. Arthi, the bolder of the two, immediately made conversation while Noorie smiled shyly. The girls chatted about their holidays and other classmates, and both Arthi and Noorie started feeling a little left out.

'Are you done?' whispered Noorie.

Arthi nodded as she gulped down the last mouthful.

'Let's go then,' said Noorie.

The girls said goodbye and left towards the Yellow Dorm. They walked in companionable silence until they reached the corridors facing the courtyard. It was just as crowded as before.

'I don't want to go back to the dorm. The bed just reminds me of the fact that I'm here alone,' scowled Arthi.

Noorie understood exactly what she was feeling. She suggested they stay outside in the corridor instead. The weather was pleasant and they could just stand around near the wooden railings and watch the rest of the students come in with their parents. The two girls found a good spot to people-watch and time slipped by. They occasionally made comments and observations and even poked fun at a few odd dresses and haircuts. Both of them were trying really hard not to think of home.

Suddenly the wail of a police siren rang through the air and almost everyone stopped what they were doing and wondered what was happening. From their height, the girls could see a motorcade making its way through the boulevard of tall trees into the courtyard. Led by two policemen in motorcycles, a black Jeep with a flashing, screaming siren, a shiny, white Mercedes-Benz slid to a halt in the centre of the courtyard. Arthi and Noorie watched open-mouthed as did everyone else. The policemen jumped out and stood to attention. Two men completely attired in black jumped out of a jeep behind the Mercedes and opened the door of the car. The girls craned their neck to get the first glimpse, but the door was blocking their view.

They watched as a regal woman wrapped in a cream sari embellished with gold stepped out of the car. Her hair was silvery white and her beautiful face was lined. She paused as she took in the people around her and then walked ahead gracefully. Two senior girls ran down the steps and greeted her. They then proceeded to bend down and touch her feet with their fingertips while her fingers brushed over their bent heads.

'Wow! What was that?' asked Noorie.

'She looks like a queen or something,' replied Arthi.

In their excitement, they almost missed the tall girl dressed in a powder-blue skirt and jacket who was stepping out of the Mercedes. She walked over to her family members, mimicking the same graceful gait as the older woman's.

'If *that* lady is her mum, she is *really* old!' exclaimed Arthi.

'Shh! Not so loud! Maybe it's her grandmum?' said Noorie.

'How old do you think she is?' asked Arthi, looking at the girl.

'Our age, probably? Or maybe a year older? She is quite tall, isn't she?'

'Come on, let's go back to the dormitory and see if she is coming there.'

The girls left their view-posts and ran to the Yellow Dorm. While they waited, they met a few more of their classmates. The girls were right in the middle of a discussion of who their class teacher might be this year when the door swung open and in walked three men in black carrying matching brown leather suitcases. The chitchat in the dorm became a hushed silence as the stately old lady and her entourage entered the Yellow Dorm.

Annie Nanny ran forward and bowed down low to her, and she smiled, saying something to her softly. The girls watched avidly as Annie Nanny said something and made some gestures, finally pointing in their direction.

'I think she is coming here,' whispered Arthi.

The entourage made its way to the row where the new girls had settled in. They didn't know why, but when the old lady approached the bed near Noorie, they all jumped up and stood at attention.

'Hello, girls! My granddaughter Sreedevi will be joining your class this year. Now whose bed is this?' she asked sweetly.

'Mm-mine,' stammered Noorie in awe.

Up close, the lady was even taller and more impressive, and Noorie caught a whiff of something very exotic and expensive from her.

'Aha! And what is your name, dear?'

'Noorie.'

'Hmm . . . Sreedevi, come here, child. Meet Noorie. She is going to be sleeping in the next bed. And what about you girls? What are your names?' she commanded.

The girls quickly parroted their names breathlessly to a quiet Sreedevi, who nodded slightly after each name.

'So, the nanny will help you unpack. I will be leaving now. I have a meeting to attend at the Fern Hill Palace Hotel, Sree,' she concluded.

Sreedevi nodded and then bent down and touched her feet. As she stood up, her grandmother embraced her briskly and then left the room followed by her guards.

The girls stood around feeling a little odd and ill at ease. It was like they knew Sreedevi was somehow different from them but they couldn't quite put their finger on it.

Arthi, ever the outspoken one, questioned Sreedevi, 'So what meeting does your grandmother have to attend?'

'It's confidential,' replied Sreedevi, her nose rising an inch in the air.

Arthi didn't like being snubbed. She made a face and turned away.

'Where are you from?' enquired Jenna.

'Kashmir,' replied Sreedevi, looking around the room with evident disappointment.

'And you have relatives studying in the school as well?'

'Yes, cousins.'

The conversation felt forced and so Jenna clamped down as well.

Arthi signalled to Noorie and they left the dorm into the warmth of the playground outside. They discussed the new girl as they walked around in the lush, green grass. Around them, younger children were playing happily on swings, see-saws, and jungle gyms. Huge eucalyptus trees towered behind and the air smelt faintly medicinal. They talked about everything except home and their parents. Soon, Jenna, Radhica, and Savita joined them and they continued talking about their possible teachers.

Night fell early in the mountains. By seven o'clock, darkness set in. Most of the girls were from the plains and were used to long, sunny days and late dinners at eight or nine o'clock. So supper at six o'clock was something Arthi and Noorie were not expecting. Noorie wondered if she would even be hungry after her enormous tea. But when she reached the dining hall and was engulfed in the warmth and aroma of a promising meal, she felt a rumble in her tummy.

'Ooh! Delicious! Chapattis and chicken curry!' exclaimed Radhica.

She had an eye for good food and always appreciated it.

'And look! For pudding we have a chocolate soufflé! Yummy!'

Both Noorie and Arthi were impressed by the food. The chicken curry was hot, spicy, and extremely delicious. And pudding after dinner was not something they were used to, so the soufflé was an instant hit!

'If the food here is this great, I think I'm going to get fat!' announced Arthi. 'Is it like this every day or what?'

'Mostly! Of course, I hate the vegetables, but other than that, it's all right. The best part is the puddings. The sister in the kitchen who makes them is a wiz,' said Jenna between mouthfuls.

'Wonder where Sreedevi is?' said Noorie, suddenly remembering her neighbour.

'Who cares? She seems like a total snob!' said Arthi.

'But she's pretty, no?' said Savita suddenly.

'Oh no! Here we go again!' said Radhica, looking exasperated.

'What? Why can't you, girls, appreciate beauty?' replied Savita.

Arthi and Noorie looked puzzled until Radhica explained while Savita protested. Savita was apparently a great admirer of good looks. She always picked her friends based on how pretty they were. The same applied to teachers as well. She studied well for the subjects that were taught by pretty ones while the ordinary-looking teachers dealt with a lazy Savita who couldn't care less. Noorie laughed hearing this and earned a stern stare from Savita.

'So this year it's going to be Madam Sreedevi, is it?' asked Arthi.

'Oh! Stop it, girls! If Jenna is friendly with someone new, no one finds fault, but when I do, why is it wrong? And if she happens to be pretty, so what? It's not a *crime* to be beautiful!' said Savita.

The girls hooted with laughter at that, and Savita left the table in a huff.

'She'll come around,' said Radhica, still laughing.

The crisp mountain breeze tugged at the girls' sweaters as they made their way back to their dorms. Laughing senior girls went upstairs to their dorms and cubies while the younger children went off to the Pink and Red dorms. The night sky was blue-black and dotted with stars and a crescent moon. A few lights twinkled here and there on the surrounding mountains like bits and pieces of a necklace.

Annie nanny instructed them to wash and change into their nighties or pyjamas. Both Arthi and Noorie had flannel pyjamas with ridiculous bunnies on them. They laughed as they saw their identical nightclothes. Obviously their parents had bought them from the same store in Ooty the previous day. Sreedevi was already dressed for bed in a fuchsia satin nightie with frills and puffed arms. Arthi snorted with laughter. She thought she looked like a cupcake with icing. Savita had magically appeared at her bedside, and the two were smiling and giggling about something.

'Probably *our* clothes,' thought Noorie.

'Why is she wearing something like that? It's something a movie star would wear? Maybe she is one!' said Arthi when they got away from the bed.

Noorie just giggled as she brushed her teeth.

'In your beds in five minutes, girls!' yelled Annie Nanny.

'But it's only seven thirty!' exclaimed Arthi.

'Lights out in five minutes!'

'This is crazy! I can't sleep so early! I usually sleep at nine or ten at night!' she continued.

Scowling and complaining, the girls made their way to their beds. Most of them were under their covers by the time the lights went out. Noorie shivered as she crept into her cold bed. Her toes felt numb and she rubbed her legs, trying to get warm. She was used to warm, balmy nights, not shivery ones like these. Slowly the dorm became quiet. A few coughs and sniffles could be heard here and there. Noorie squinted and looked over at Arthi's bed. She was very still and definitely asleep in spite of all her earlier claims about not being tired. She looked over to the other side, where Sreedevi lay with her back towards her. Noorie sighed, feeling very lonely. She slept alone at home but somehow this loneliness was very different. She wanted to be angry with her parents for sending her away. But right now she only missed them deeply. What she wouldn't give for a smile from her sweet, soft mother or a booming laugh from her big, strong father now.

# Chapter 4

# MYRA

Myra looked at her reflection in the mirror one last time before leaving her bedroom. She straightened her smart brown blazer and ran her long, slender fingers over the golden yellow embroidery on the pocket. It was the seal and motto of the new school that she was joining. She had spent the last years in Highcliffe preparatory school and she had loved it there. But now that she was starting class 7, she would have to move to a bigger school as Highcliffe only went up till class 6. She had heard a lot about the Royal Academy for Women from her neighbours and a few family friends. It was known as a very posh, fancy school that was very hard to get admission into. Her grandfather's connections in the local community and the fact that her father was a very well-renowned and well-respected doctor had given her application the momentum it needed to be accepted. Everyone was thrilled that she got in, but she felt odd going to a new school and starting all over again. None of her old classmates would be coming to this school. Almost all of them had joined Glendale Higher Secondary just down the road, and she wished her parents were sending her there instead.

She sighed as she adjusted the white ribbons in her long, light brown plaits. Her lovely hazel-brown eyes looked sad and her pretty rosebud mouth was downturned. She picked up her schoolbag and went downstairs to see her family already busy with breakfast. Her grandfather was digging into his parathas with the vigour one wouldn't expect to see in an eighty-year-old. She smiled to seen his expression of absolute joy as he savoured his food. Her father was talking on the phone; as usual, it was a call from the hospital and it looked like he would skip breakfast yet again as he rushed over to save someone else's life. Her mother bustled about in the kitchen and came back into the living room carrying a plate laden with hot, sizzling parathas. She was a lawyer but she had never worked. She had stayed home to take care of Myra and her younger sister, who was just three years old now. Her little sister Sara was a mirror image of their mother: a head full of curly black hair, snow-white complexion with rosy cheeks and smiling black eyes. She even had her merry disposition and gentle manners.

'All set to go to your school, *jan*?' asked her mother as she placed a paratha on her plate.

Myra nodded shakily. Her grandfather looked up and his wrinkled face became even more lined as he smiled and winked at her. He was her confidant. She told him everything: all the good and the bad and the ugly too. So he knew very well about her apprehensions about this new school and her dream of joining Glendale like her other friends. He had tried to alleviate her fears and worries but she was still nervous and jittery.

Her father finished his call and sat down to join them. He smiled at Myra and complimented her on her new uniform.

'I'll be dropping you off in school today Myra-*jan*,' he said. 'I know Sr. Rosemary, the principal, and so I'll pop into her office as well.'

Myra was surprised but pleased. Her *Abba* was a very busy man. It was usually her *Ammi* who dropped her and picked her up and did all the errands at home. The fact that Abba was taking the time out of his busy schedule to take her to school on her very first day made her feel very important. *Or maybe he just had to meet Sr. Rosemary and that's why he's coming?* She thought suddenly and her bubble of joy deflated a little. She pondered about this as she chewed her paratha, lost in thought.

'Come on, Myra! It's time to go!' said her father, standing up quickly.

Myra washed up and ran to the car with her school bag after giving her ammi and grandfather kisses. The drive to the school was a quiet one. He father was concentrating on the road. Myra looked around with interest at the new surroundings. They were moving into a quieter and more exclusive part of the town. There were fewer buildings and more trees as the car climbed the hill that led to her new school. The enormous grey gate was open, and eucalyptus, pines, fir, and a few other trees she didn't know loomed on either side of the freshly tarred road.

'They don't even have any potholes here!' she thought. The roads in the town had quite a few massive ones, and she and her father always joked that one of these days they would fall inside one and never get out again. They were getting deeper and deeper each year, and with the rains due in a few weeks, Myra imagined what a mess the Ooty town would be.

The large courtyard was littered with school buses and a few cars. Children of varying ages were getting out of the brown and cream school buses, laughing and chatting. They looked so at home and Myra felt a hint of panic. She knew no one here! She gulped as she followed her father up the stone steps. She took in the creamy walls with their fresh coat of paint. The dark-brown polished wooden floors gleamed under her new black Bata shoes. The ceilings were high, and she felt she was entering something like a church or cathedral. Everything here seemed out of proportion to what she was used to. Her cottage was a modest one with tiny rooms, and her old school building looked like a ruin next to this magnificent school complex. Her panic rose as she stood outside the principal's office with her father. She slowly slipped her hand into his and clutched it like a lifeline. *Even the flowers in the garden looked bigger and brighter!* She took a deep breath and told herself to calm down and stop acting silly.

'You can go in now,' said the kind white-haired secretary.

Myra followed her father into a large room with minimal furnishings. It was quite a contrast to the grandeur and opulence outside. A simple cross hung on the wall and there were no other paintings or pictures on the walls. A severe-looking woman sat across the desk attired in a black veil and white tunic.

'Dr Sheikh! To what do I owe this pleasure?' said a smiling Sr. Rosemary as she nodded at them to take their seats.

Myra couldn't help staring at the woman's odd face. It was round and chubby with a pinkish complexion. Her eyes were small and so was her nose. Her lips were a thin straight line, like she kept them pursed all the time. But it was her facial hair that Myra was most fascinated by. Her eyebrows were so faint that they were practically non-existent; however, a thin line of dark fuzz rested between her nose and lips, like a moustache. A few strands of dark hair sprung out from a mole to the side of her chin. And when she smiled, she didn't look kind; she looked a little menacing. Myra gulped, thinking about the kind grandfatherly face of her old principal.

But her father seemed at ease, talking and laughing with the nun. He introduced a silent Myra to the principal, who ignored her almost immediately and focused on her father instead.

'Clearly she thinks my abba is amazing,' thought Myra, rolling her eyes inwardly.

'She is a very nice woman,' said her abba once they were out of the scary woman's office.

Myra was thankful for the sunshine, birds, and flowers suddenly. The nun's spartan office had unnerved her. She didn't quite agree with her father on his comment but she held her tongue.

'Now you find your class and make some new friends. It will be all right!' he said, kissing her on the top of her head before heading back to the car. Myra stood by the brown railings, watching her tall, handsome father make his way through the crowd of children.

Myra had always been afraid of trying something new. New places, new people—why, even new food terrified her! She wished she were like her father in that regard. He was always so brave and confident even when people were mean or rude to him. And she had seen some of his patients in his clinic; they were quite nasty if they weren't cured as fast as *they* wanted to. But he took their sharp words in his stride and continued treating them with respect. His kindness and compassion always amazed her. But sometimes she felt he was doing it to be *liked*, to *fit in better* with the community here in Ooty, because after all, they were not locals; they were Kashmiris who moved here in the 1960s at the height of the tensions with Pakistan.

Their ancestral home was in a little village near Muzaffarabad in what was now Pakistan-occupied Kashmir (POK). It now lay to the west of Jammu and Kashmir and was a self-governing state under Pakistan. Her great-grandfather and his brothers had owned several farms where they had cultivated apples, cherries, and walnuts. They also had several heads of cattle and sheep. When a part of Kashmir broke away and became Azad Kashmir, also known as POK, her grandfather had been studying in Srinagar. He had believed in the Lion of Kashmir, Sheikh Abdullah, and he wanted to continue living in India. So he left behind his family home and moved away from all he knew. It had been a difficult period for her grandfather but he soon met and married her grandmother, who was from Srinagar itself. Her father was born a few years later and they moved to Delhi and then they had moved down south to Ooty, where her grandfather set up his business selling Kashmiri handicrafts, wooden work, and pashmina shawls to both locals and tourists. Her mother had grown up in Delhi but she moved to the south after their marriage. It was big change for her Ammi as she spoke no Tamil like her Abba, just Koshur, Hindi, and English. But over the years, she had learnt the language and now she spoke Tamil quite fluently, though with a funny accent which Abba teased her about.

Sometimes Myra wondered what she was. *Was she a Kashmiri? Or a Tamil?* She didn't quite know. A little voice would nag her at night, worrying her. She consoled herself, saying that she was Indian at the end of the day and it didn't matter what her origins were. She said the pledge at assembly every day and sang the national anthem, 'Jana Gana Mana', with as much pride as her neighbours and friends. Of course she was *Indian* to the core!

# Chapter 5

# SETTLING IN

'*Good morning, girls!*'
Sr. Molly's cheery greeting resonated throughout the massive study hall. The new girls jumped in their seats, obviously not used to this high-powered greeting. The old girls responded with an even louder 'Good morning!' and wide smiles. Sr. Molly was the study hall supervisor and extremely popular with all students. Born in England but having spent most of her adult life serving the mission in India, Sr. Molly was more Indian than British by the time she celebrated her sixtieth birthday the previous year. With twinkling blue eyes and a mile-wide smile on her face, she took her seat on the raised platform and eyed the girls, juniors and seniors, old and new with a keen eye. Though she was kind-hearted, she wasn't someone who tolerated any sort of cheekiness.

The study hall, with its high ceiling and wooden panelling, was a sombre room. All students from the age of ten until sixteen were assigned desks and lockers where they placed their books and conducted their studies while in the boarding. The room had a hushed atmosphere and was almost entirely lit by low-hanging chandeliers that gave off a bright yellow glow. Rows of ancient teakwood desks and chairs stood like tired sentries from wall to wall.

Noorie inspected her ancient desk and chair. There were a few scribbles and ink marks and she thought they gave the desk character. She tried to read and could just about make out a few words—'Shagun', 'JJ sucks', 'Beware of the Nazi'. It made no sense to her. She looked around for Arthi and found her at the end of the row behind her. She was seated between Jenna and Radhica and for that she was grateful. With every passing hour, she was feeling more and more unsettled by the new faces around her. She peered over her shoulder to have another look at Arthi. She was in deep conversation with a cheeky-looking girl whom she wasn't familiar with. Noorie wished she were as outgoing and confident as Arthi, who seemed to settle in with little difficulty.

After an hour of morning studies, the girls made their way to the school buildings that lay at the opposite end of the horseshoe layout. Class 7 was located on the second floor of the weathered ivory-coloured building at the far end which was the multipurpose block. Noorie walked with Jenna and Radhica, who quickly filled her in about the different teachers and their characteristic traits.

'Watch out for Ms Pavan. She takes Hindi and she is very tough.'

'Don't worry about geography, if it's Ms Anita's, then she is a darling. She gives lots of free periods.'

'Never, ever mess with Ms Sindhu. She can rip you apart with her tongue.'

The sage advice continued all the way to the class, and Noorie listened avidly and gulped inwardly in terror. The class teacher was already there when they arrived. She was new but didn't look very intimidating.

'Come on, girls! Take your seats fast. Hurry up, ma!' she urged.

'God! Her accent is funny!' giggled Radhica quietly.

'Shh! Be quiet! She is right there and can hear you, idiot!' chided Jenna.

Noorie did find the tone and accent a little odd and unfamiliar. The new teacher introduced herself as Ms Rani and she was from Ooty itself.

'That explains the accent,' mumbled Radhica snootily.

'Ssh!' hissed Jenna.

Ms Rani seemed warm and enthusiastic, which appealed quickly to the students.

'The first day will be mostly settling down, getting your books, and meeting your teachers. Tomorrow we will have regular class. But today I want to select the class leader.'

The class dissolved into excited murmurs and glances.

'Are there any volunteers?'

Noorie looked around and found more unfamiliar faces. Probably the day scholars, she thought. She wondered who would volunteer for the job. In her old school, the job of the class leader had been tedious and not even a little fun. She was surprised to find several hands pop up around the class. Near her, both Jenna and Radhica had their hands up and were almost out of their seats in enthusiasm.

'Lovely! What an enthusiastic bunch you are! Now how many of you have previously been class leaders?' asked Ms Rani.

Half the hands went down and a few scowls appeared. Radhica's hand went limp and Jenna gave a smug smile as she kept her hand raised.

'Good! Good! Since you girls have already had the chance of proving your leadership qualities, I think it would be fair if we gave the others a chance this time. What do you say? So let's see once again the girls who would like to be the class leader especially since they have never given it a go before.'

Groans and mutterings broke out, and different sets of hands were in the air now. Jenna was dejected while Radhica looked radiant. There were six girls in contention for the post: three boarders and three day scholars. Ms Rani wrote down their names on the blackboard.

'And now we will vote,' she said.

The girls broke into excited squeals and giggles. They had never done this before. Normally the class teacher just picked one of the girls, but this was proving to be an interesting morning for all. One by one, the candidates were made to stand up while Ms Rani called out for supporters to raise their hands. Then a count was taken and written against the name on the board. Noorie and Arthi raised their hands for Radhica as they were unfamiliar with the others. And much to their delight, she won the vote. Jenna grudgingly congratulated her and then sat silently in her seat, sulking. The other boarders came over to pat Radhica on her back and shake her hands. Noorie still couldn't understand what the big deal was about. The day scholars sulked in a corner, huddling around their candidates and giving Radhica dirty looks.

'What's the deal with the day scholars?' asked Noorie to Radhica.

'Oh! We don't get along with them,' she replied simply.

'All of them?'

'Yeah. I don't even know why. It's just something the seniors do and we just kinda follow?'

'But why? I mean, are they mean to us or something?'

'Not particularly. But it's been like that since I joined this school. As far as I know, it's always been that way. We keep to our side always. It's not like we go all out and fight with them or something. But we don't really make any friendships with them.'

Noorie was confused by this outright dislike and distrust of the day scholars. They looked like a bunch of ordinary girls to her, and she couldn't understand what the fuss was all about. But then again she was just a new girl and she didn't want to upset the balance, so she chose to stay silent.

The rest of the day was a blur of new faces, new books, and understanding the class timetable. The new girls were trying to keep up with the old ones as they fell into an easy camaraderie. By the end of the day Arthi, Noorie, and Sreedevi were all looking a little lost and overwhelmed as they gathered their bags and left for the boarding.

Noorie wolfed down her hot and crumbly chicken puff at teatime. Food had always comforted her, and now more than any other time, she sought its assistance.

'So how was your first day?' asked Jenna as she buttered her toast.

'Scary,' replied Noorie honestly.

The other girls had yet to arrive at the table. It was just the two of them now.

'Hey, did you feel bad about the whole class-leader elections?' asked Noorie.

'Nah! Not really! I didn't even want it actually,' replied Jenna, brushing off her embarrassment.

Noorie just nodded quietly. She could see that Jenna was still upset about it. She had obviously wanted the position, but if she chose to deny it now, Noorie didn't want to ruffle her feathers unnecessarily.

Savita burst into the dining hall and rushed to their table. She quickly looked around looking for someone and then, satisfied that they were not there, she gathered Jenna and Noorie into a huddle.

'Girls! You are not going to believe this?' she whispered excitedly.

'What?' said Jenna, her mouth full of butter.

'We have a royal in our class! A real princess!' said Savita, jumping up and down in her seat.

'Psht! What bull!' replied Jenna even though her eyes were as round as saucers on their table.

'Who is it?' asked Noorie, suddenly looking around with interest.

'Sreedevi, of course!' replied Savita, looking at Noorie in exasperation. 'Come on! Nobody in our class has that kind of grandeur. It's obvious even to the blind.'

'Who told you all this?' asked Jenna.

'She did, silly!' replied Savita with glee. 'She told me that she is related to the Kashmir royal family. Isn't that amazing? A real princess! Have you ever seen one before?'

Both Jenna and Noorie were too stunned to speak. Noorie was even more hushed as she realized she was sleeping right next to royalty. She felt a little dizzy just then and she hoped that Sreedevi didn't find her too smelly or dirty or common. She was suddenly very conscious of herself. Just then Sreedevi walked in through the swinging dining hall doors and the three girls gazed at her in awe. She did hold herself with remarkable dignity and grace, bordering on haughtiness. She held her chin up slightly and walked with her aquiline nose up in the air. She took her seat at her table and looked down at her chicken puff and sighed, looking decidedly unhappy about it.

'What are you girls staring at?' asked Arthi, and all three of them jumped up. They had been so engrossed in watching Sreedevi they hadn't seen her. Noorie quickly brought her up to speed with what was going on but Arthi was far from impressed.

'I don't see what the big deal is. There are hundreds of royals in India—after all, we had so many princely states with so many kings and queens. I'm sure there are other princesses in the school as well. Didn't the welcome kit say so?' she said, munching her apple with gusto.

'She just seems like any of us to me. Nothing special,' she continued, shrugging.

Savita didn't like the fact that Arthi had just burst their bubble, and she left the table in a huff to join

Sreedevi, who gave her a warm smile as she sat down beside her.

The bell rang out and beckoned the girls to the study hall for an hour of evening studies under the keen eye of Ms Vasanta. Attired in her trademark dark sweater and pink woollen bonnet, Ms Vasanta made sure all the girls had their noses firmly in their books for an hour even though it was just the first day of school. She insisted they go over the first chapter of whatever textbooks they had. The hour stretched on painfully, and the girls sighed with relief when the bell rang, announcing the end of their torture session. The girls left the study hall and gathered near the bell.

'I have never *ever* looked at a book on my first day of school,' grumbled Arthi.

'Me neither,' replied Noorie.

'So what's next?' asked Arthi.

'We have some time until supper and then it's food and bed,' replied Jenna.

Arthi was done with her brushing and washing before the others in Yellow Dorm. She got under her blankets and looked around the girls near her, each one busy with her own thing. Some were changing into their pyjamas, others were whispering and laughing, and some were sitting in their beds, saying their prayers. She thought of her home suddenly. A sharp stab of pain made her cringe as she saw her mother's smiling face and heard her tinkling laughter. She smelt Shanti Akka's ghee dosa and missed her warm hugs. A lump formed in her throat and her eyes began to water. She quickly slid under her blankets and covered her head with her pillow, sobbing quietly under it. She wondered what her mother was up to just then. *Is she lonely too? Is Appa back? Will they make up or is this the end?* What would happen to her? Would it be the same growing up with one parent instead of two? So many important things were happening back home; things that would have such a profound impact on her life and she wasn't even there. She was a mere spectator now.

The girls soon fell into the strict regimen implemented by the nuns. A typical day was as follows:

- Wake-up call at 6.00 a.m.
- Prayers in the assembly hall at 7 a.m.
- Breakfast at 7.15 a.m.
- Morning studies from 8.00 a.m.–9.00 a.m.
- Assembly in school at 9.15 a.m.
- Class begins at 9.30 am
- Lunch break at 1.00 p.m.
- Class resumes at 2.00 p.m.
- Class ends at 4.30 p.m.
- Sports/arts/music/dance and other extracurricular activities for an hour and then back to the boarding.

Slowly Noorie and Arthi interacted with their many classmates in the boarding, liking a few and disliking a few too. Usha was one such girl they both took an instant dislike to. She was a disproportionately built girl, with thin shoulders, wide hips, and skinny legs. She had small, ratty eyes that darted left and right all the time, giving her a shifty look. And she had a nasty tongue that she wasn't shy to use. They both steered clear of her. But in general they liked their classmates.

Jenna was a sweet person who was always ready to lend a helping hand. Radhica was full of energy and fun even though she tried to be strict with everyone as she was the class leader and the role demanded her to monitor the others when the teacher wasn't around. Savita was around Sreedevi the whole time, and two of them kept to themselves most of the time, doing their hair and painting their nails or flipping through Sreedevi's fashion magazines. Seema and Gayathri were best buddies. They were both from Coorg and did exceptionally well in sports. And then there was Priya, who was the class clown and prankster. She barely sat still in class and was always reading books filled with jokes, puzzles, and pranks. Jenna told them that Priya had been in a lot of trouble last year and had almost been expelled, so this year she was trying to lie low.

Meenu, who always had her nose buried in a book, was the class topper. She apparently hadn't watched a movie in the last five years, according to Priya, but Noorie was sure she was bluffing. The new girls didn't really make an effort to get to know the day scholars. They just learnt their names and made polite conversation occasionally. The two groups largely kept to themselves.

Now the teachers were another matter altogether. There were some good ones and some very scary ones. Ms Rani was one of the good ones. She was kind but firm and she was quite popular among her girls. The maths teacher Ms Sindhu was a white-haired, highly respected individual in their school. She was an alumnus who had returned to serve her alma mater after completing her master's in mathematics from a reputed university in Madras. She rewarded hard work and had no patience for whiners or slackers. The science teacher Ms Bartley was a petite woman engulfed in a large black shawl that flapped around her as she walked. Her loud booming voice had amazed the girls the first time they heard her. She spoke very fast and insisted they take notes while she taught for she didn't believe in the textbook. Her notes were far more extensive and in-depth and her question papers were set based on these.

Both Noorie and Arthi were above-average students and they settled into the new curriculum with relative ease. The pace was quick and the teachers expected their students to participate in class and complete their homework, projects, and assignments on time. The girls were soon busy with homework and tests, and before they knew it, a month had gone by.

# Chapter 6

# THE VISITOR

E very Saturday the girls were given letter paper to pen down the news for their folks back home. They could write to their parents or grandparents and even to their older siblings. They were given an 'inland' for domestic mail or the aerogramme if their parents lived overseas. Noorie looked forward to it while Arthi detested the whole exercise.

'I don't know what to say!' she groaned as she watched Noorie enviously.

'Just tell them all that has happened over the week,' replied Noorie.

The light-blue inland was filled with Noorie's small, neat cursive handwriting as she regaled her parents with stories from the previous week. She wrote to them about the new friends she was making, the teachers she was fond of, the food she ate, and the tests she did well in. Noorie reread the letter she had received last week from her mother, and she tried to make sure she answered all her questions about school. Her father had just penned two lines at the end, saying he hoped she was doing her best to make him proud.

The first time Noorie had received a letter from home, she was surprised to see it had already been opened. And then one of the older girls had explained that Sr. Josephine read all their mail! This lack of privacy unnerved her a little. *What if she wanted to write a complaint about the school or teachers or Sr. Josephine herself? How would she?* She hoped it wouldn't come to that.

Arthi stared and stared at her blank letter paper. She just didn't have a way with words. She knew what she wanted to write but she just couldn't bring herself to do it. Arthi hadn't received any letters from home yet and she was desperate for news about her amma but she didn't have the nerve to ask about it. So she tried to write mundane things into the letter half-heartedly while she waited anxiously for good news even though she had no idea what *good* was any more. *Is it better they were together or apart?*

Just then one of the senior girls who was minding the phone in the boarding burst into the buzzing study hall and yelled, 'Arthi, new girl! Phone call!'

Arthi was jolted out of her reverie. She threw down the inland and pen and ran all the way to Sr. Josephine's office.

'Amma?' she gasped into the phone, out of breath.

'Arthi! How are you, kanna? All OK?' her mother replied.

Arthi closed her eyes and savoured the sound of her mother's voice. It had been a month since she had heard from her.

'Why didn't you call me last week?' she complained.

'I've been trying every Sunday but this phone is always engaged!'

'Ah! OK.'

There was a moment of silence as both of them collected their thoughts.

'So? How are you, Amma? How is everything?' asked Arthi nervously.

'All fine this side, dear. Work is going on well and I'm busy. The house is empty without you, and Shanti Akka talks about you every day,' laughed her mother.

'And Appa?'

There was a long pause and Arthi kicked herself for saying those two words.

'He is fine, I think. We trying to work something out and it's . . . it's challenging,' replied her mother, her voice strained.

'So are you enjoying the school? Do you like it there?' she asked, swiftly changing the subject and giving Arthi something else to talk about.

They spoke for another ten minutes before the senior girl started staring at Arthi and making gestures to cut the call, which she did reluctantly.

'You know, the communications system here is terrible! Why can't they allow phone calls on all days of the week? And why can't they have ten lines or something! I mean, isn't this a posh and fancy school? Why don't they let us receive phone call every day?' complained Arthi as she sat down next to Noorie.

'At least be happy you got one phone call. I haven't received any so far!'

Arthi was suddenly grateful that she was able to speak to her mother after one whole month. With hundreds of parents trying to reach their kids, it was indeed a minor miracle to get a phone call.

'Arthi, there is someone here to see you! Go to Sr. Josephine's office right away,' yelled the senior girl from the telephone.

'Wow! A phone call and a visitor? You lucky thing!' said Noorie, green-eyed with jealousy.

Arthi got up excitedly and walked swiftly to the office. She wondered who it could be. Her mother was in Madras and her grandparents were too worn-out to travel all the way to Ooty. She knocked on the enormous door and was called in. Her visitor turned to look at her as she entered, and Arthi stood stock-still by the door as she locked eyes with her father.

Sr. Josephine had a very smug smile on her face.

'Come, child,' she gestured warmly.

Arthi sat down gingerly in the seat opposite the nun and nodded at her father, who was looking at her with a strange smile. She didn't know what to do. *Was she supposed to hug him or greet him or what?*

'So, normally I don't allow visitors except at midterm when you have a free weekend. But since your father has come all the way here just to see you as he didn't get a chance to say goodbye when you left, I couldn't refuse him. And that too having such an important business,' the nun gushed.

'I can't let you go out to the town. You can spend an hour or two in the school premises itself. There is a parlour where guests can be entertained. Sunita, the girl outside, will show you,' she concluded, nodding at Appa.

Arthi's father thanked the nun warmly and then proceeded to compliment her on the furnishing in her room, at which the nun blushed happily. He went on and on about school's reputation and said it was because of their dedicated service that such fine young women were created.

The father and daughter sat facing each other on giant dark-brown leather armchairs in the guest parlour. Arthi couldn't remember the last time she had spent time alone with her father. She decided to let him take the lead and understand why he was here. She didn't believe he had come just to *see* her. *What was he up to?*

'So, Arthi, how are you enjoying the school?'

Arthi mumbled something about it being good and that she was settling down.

'And the teachers? I hope they are as good as can be expected from a school of this stature,' her father continued.

She nodded not sure how she was supposed to rate her own teachers, especially since she had known them for barely a month.

They sat in silence for a few moments, looking at each other, sizing each other up until Arthi finally looked away and started looking at the carpet instead.

'Well, your mother and I are going to part ways. I'm sure she has told you about it. I don't particularly care about what she does but I am sure about one thing, I will take custody of you,' said her father.

Arthi looked up, startled; she was too shocked to say anything. *What did he mean? That she would have to live with him? That she wouldn't be allowed to be with her mother?*

'But . . . I . . . I thought . . .' she stammered.

'I know what you thought. But that's not going to happen. You are my child, you have my surname, and you will live with me. You can continue studying in this school, but when it's holidays, you will come to my house and live with your grandparents in Tirunelveli.'

Arthi started hyperventilating. *What was happening? Why was her world crumbling? She didn't even like her paternal grandparents. They were so traditional and orthodox. And her mother? What about her?*

'And Amma?' she whispered through her tears.

'She can go to hell for all I care!' he spat.

Arthi felt numb. Tears rolled down her cheeks but she could barely feel them. She wanted to scream and say no, but a giant lump had settled in her throat, making it hard for her to speak. She just sat like a mute lost to the world around her.

'Well, I am leaving now,' announced her father standing up after a few minutes.

Arthi kept her head down, a million thoughts churning in her mind. She said nothing, just continued sitting there, for she didn't have the will to get up. The heavy wooden door burst open after what seemed an eternity to her.

'Hey! You're still here? I saw your dad leaving awhile back!' exclaimed Sunita, the senior who showed her in.

Arthi just nodded without really seeing her. She was trying to make sense of what had just happened. *Could he really do all he said? Take custody of her? Wouldn't her mother fight for her? Would she be left to his mercy?*

'Would it be possible for me to make a call?' she asked hoarsely.

'What?' replied Sunita, surprised.

'A phone call. I want to call my mother,' whispered Arthi.

'We aren't allowed to make any calls here. We only receive them but you could try and talk to Sr. Josephine.'

Arthi walked over to Sr. Josephine's office but it was locked. She must have left for lunch, she thought as she looked at her watch. The peals of the school bell interrupted her thoughts and she slowly made her way to the dining hall. She was quiet during lunch and didn't say anything even though Jenna and Noorie kept nagging her. She went back to Sr. Josephine's office after lunch but it was still locked. She learned that she wouldn't return until teatime and so she went back to the study hall and tried to keep herself occupied with a storybook but the words just kept swimming before her eyes.

When the bell rang for tea, Arthi rushed to the dining hall and gulped down the cookies on her plate, not because she was hungry but because she didn't want to get into trouble for missing tea. She then ran back to Sr. Josephine's office, hoping and praying she would be there. *If only she could speak to her mother and ask her if it was all true. If she could just hear from her that no one could take her away from her amma. Just one phone call and she could put out the fire burning in her heart.*

She almost cried with relief when she saw that the door was unlocked. She knocked and stepped into the room with a sense of urgency.

'Yes, what is it, child?' snapped Sr. Josephine.

She had been busy reading the children's letters and making corrections with her pencil.

'Sister, I would like to call my mother, please,' said Arthi.

Sr. Josephine's pencil paused in mid-air for a moment and then she sighed, shaking her head.

'Your father told me you would ask for this.'

'Please, Sister. I just want to make one phone call,' said Arthi, her voice breaking.

'Child, she is in the hospital. You are not to disturb her. She cannot take any call now, you understand. You must let her recover in peace.'

'In the hospital? What . . . what do you mean?' gasped Arthi.

'Ah! I shouldn't have said anything!'

'Why is she in the hospital? Did something happen to her? Please let me call home! Let me speak to her! Please!' sobbed Arthi.

Sr. Josephine looked at her with thinly veiled irritation. She had no patience for drama and emotions, and with a school full of girls, she had seen plenty of both.

'She is fine! She just had a fall and now she is recovering in the hospital. She will be fine. She will call you next week for sure. Now wipe your face and go for evening studies.'

Arthi had been dismissed with little sympathy and she now stood outside the office, her face streaked with tears, wondering what to do next. *Was her mother really in the hospital? But she had just spoken to her, hadn't she? She hadn't said anything about a fall. Was it all a lie her father concocted to prevent the nun from letting her contact her mother?*

Arthi just walked around the front courtyard, seething with anger. *It was just one phone call, one phone call!* The thought kept going over and over in her mind. She had to find a way to contact her mother, but how? The phone was unavailable and all letters were read and reread by the horrid nun. If only she could get a letter out in secret to her mother, asking her all these questions in her mind. But how could she do that? None of them left the campus, and she couldn't get out and do it herself. She had no idea where the postbox or even post office was. And she had no inlands or stamps? And she didn't even have any money to buy it. She stamped her feet frustrated at her helplessness. For all its poshness, this stupid school didn't allow her a phone call when she needed it and they had no respect for privacy!

'Arthi! Arthi!'

Someone was yelling her name and she looked up to the corridor and saw Noorie and Jenna waving and yelling her name. She had walked to the far end of the courtyard without realizing.

'Study time! Hurry up! You'll be late!'

Arthi nodded and walked back swiftly. There was just one thought in her head now: *how to contact her mother without Sr. Josephine's knowledge.* As she sat in the study hall, staring mindlessly at her history textbook, she thought about her father and her chest contracted with hatred. *He had come all this way just to frighten her, hadn't he? To put her and her mother in place. He didn't really want her; he was just doing this to spite her mother. But what if he had been serious? What if it was true? What if she really would be carted off to Tirunelveli to live with her grandparents?* Arthi closed her eyes in horror.

'Hey! What's wrong? You've been off-colour since afternoon,' asked Noorie kindly.

'Nothing, nothing,' replied Arthi.

She wasn't ready to share her woes with anybody. She wished she had a best friend, someone who could counsel her and help her through this. But there was no one she trusted implicitly like that in this school. At least, not yet.

# Chapter 7

# DARK DAYS

The monsoon hit Ooty with a vengeance. The days were cold and wet, and the sun barely peeked out. Black cumulonimbus clouds gathered ominously in the skies and the heavens opened over Ooty. It rained with a vengeance, and the winds blew hard and fast. July and August were wet months, and in the past, there had been cyclones and landslides. The adults hoped this year would be without event.

The girls hated getting out of bed in the mornings; they shivered their way through prayers and eagerly gulped down their hot breakfasts. Everything seemed grey and sombre. For Arthi, it was just a reflection of her mental state. She continued her classes like a zombie, barely paying attention and narrowly escaping punishments from irritated teachers. Noorie noticed the change in her friend's behaviour but she didn't know what to do. She had asked her several times but Arthi just looked irritated now so Noorie left her to her own devices. She started spending more time with Radhica instead who was full of life and energy.

On the way to class that morning, they saw a group of girls crowded around one of the notice boards near the staff room. Noorie squeezed in and tried to read the notice. She just saw a list of names that included Seema and Gayathri from her class.

'What's it for?' she asked Radhica.

'Inter-school sports,' she replied.

'So Seema and Gayathri are already selected?'

'Once you are selected, you are pretty much in. They were there last year in the sub-junior category and so I guess they will continue this year as well. Why? Are you interested?' asked Radhica.

'Me? No! I've never run in my life. The only sports I play is when we have PE,' laughed Noorie.

The girls had a PE lesson later that afternoon under the keen eye of Ms Shobha, the PE teacher. Coach Rhonda, who would be training the school team for the inter-school sports, joined her. This annual event had participants from all the high schools in Nilgiris district. It was hosted at the MRC grounds in Wellington, and the athletes trained for it with passion and zeal. The school had a history of wins at the inter-school sports but lately their efforts did not bring them the victories they hoped for. So now Coach Rhonda was on the lookout for new talent and that was why she was scouting each class for new blood.

Thankfully the rain was taking a break that afternoon but it was still quite windy and chilly. The girls shivered in their T-shirts and shorts as they stood outside in the sports field. They would be playing kho-kho, which was essentially a form of running and catching. They were divided into two teams and pitted against each other. One team sat on their haunches in a horizontal line, leaving a little space between them. They faced forward and backward in an alternate fashion and were allowed to run only in the direction they faced. The aim was to catch the members of the opposite team while running in just one direction.

Arthi was in no mood to play but Ms Shobha had already rejected her request to sit out the game. She joined the team opposite Noorie sulkily and ran half-heartedly when her turn came. Noorie's team was on the run and soon they were down to just five of them. Radhica, Noorie, and three day scholars panted wildly as they ran to avoid Arthi's team, which had both Seema and Gayathri, who ran like Olympians compared to the rest of them. Savita and Sreedevi had let themselves be caught early on as they didn't want to dirty their hair and get sweaty. Radhica and Noorie had rolled their eyes at their daintiness and sniggered privately.

'Hey, slowpoke! Try and catch me!' yelled Noorie, tugging Arthi's curly locks.

Arthi, however, was in a black mood, as she always was these days and she didn't take it kindly.

'Leave me alone,' she mumbled.

But Noorie and Radhica were both feeling a little naughty and so they continued to pull her hair whenever they had a chance, much to Arthi's exasperation.

She couldn't get up and run behind the girls as it was not her turn and so she just had to endure their mischief. Noorie and Radhica laughed happily as they saw Arthi's temper rise and they refused to listen to her threats. They were happily laughing at her, standing at one end of the field when it was suddenly Arthi's turn to run and she sprang from her position like a cheetah.

'Aieeeyyaaaa!' she screamed, making Radhica and Noorie scamper in opposite directions.

Arthi ran behind Noorie, who screamed and ran as fast as her short legs could carry her. She turned around to see Arthi running, an angry bull seeing red. Coach Rhonda watched the two girls with interest. *They had potential*, she thought. She smiled, seeing Arthi finally pounce on Noorie and pulling her hair while she screamed and begged for mercy. Ms Shobha was not so impressed by their behaviour, though, and gave them both an earful about their *unladylike* behaviour.

'There was no need to pull so hard,' mumbled Noorie angrily as she rubbed her head. Both the girls were sitting at their desks in the study hall.

'Well, you started it,' replied Arthi.

'Yeah, but it was for fun! I didn't do it to pull your hair out and make you bald!' yelled Noorie.

'You're already bald. You have so little hair anyway,' snapped back Arthi.

Noorie gasped at the insult. She opened her mouth to say something but then noticed a very tall senior standing by their study hall desks, looking very amused.

'Quite a pair, aren't you?' asked the senior.

She had light-brown eyes, long shiny hair pulled back in a ponytail and looked lean and fit. The girls stood up, looking sheepish.

'I'm Shagun. And I'm assuming you are Arthi and Noorie, right?'

'Yes!' they replied in unison.

'Good! Coach Rhonda was pretty impressed by both of you today at the PE lesson. She said you had potential to be good athletes. So we will try you for various events and then see what suits you the most and train you accordingly. Sports practice will start next week and we have just two months before the finals so the training will be hard and swift. We are looking for serious athletes and I don't appreciate any mischief or kiddie stuff, OK?' asked Shagun.

The girls nodded, too stunned to speak.

'Fine then! Come to my class tomorrow during lunch break to collect your tracksuits. You can ask Gayathri and Seema for more info, OK?'

'Yes, Shagun,' said Arthi while Noorie nodded.

'And stop pulling each other's hair. You aren't six anymore!' she added as parting shot.

Noorie groaned as she sat down. Now Shagun would remember them as stupid girls who pulled each other's hair! What a terrible first impression!

Radhica and Jenna were impressed by the news while Seema and Gayathri just smirked when Noorie broke the news to her classmates.

'Why do you think they did that?' asked Noorie, 'Do you think we will be bad at it?'

'Who cares?' replied Arthi.

Noorie turned away. Lately anything she said or did made Arthi mad. She wasn't like this when they had started out. Something had happened and she had changed into this girl who seemed to permanently have a dark cloud over her head. And she had begun falling behind in her studies too. The teachers were constantly pulling up Arthi in class now for not completing her homework or missing assignments or not paying attention. But no matter what punishment was doled out, Arthi just didn't seem to care. She seemed to have shut everyone out in the last few days.

The next morning, Noorie and Arthi joined the rest of the girls dressed in their dark blue tracksuits. There was a light drizzle and the sky was overcast. Their practice would be from 7 a.m. until 9 a.m. every day for the next two months, come rain or shine.

The new girls made their way to enormous school kitchen. It was their first time there and they were awestruck. The array of smells, the size of the stoves, huge pots with steaming contents, innumerable shelves of fruits and vegetables, and the bustle of activity so early in the morning impressed them. Cooks and helpers scampered about, rushing to get breakfast on the tables.

'What are we doing here?' whispered Noorie to Arthi, who looked equally clueless.

There were several steel cups laid out in neat rows on the marble counters. Noorie picked up one and peered inside. She reared back in disgust when she saw a raw egg wobbling inside the cup. Her surprise rose when she saw one of the helpers behind the counter pour hot, steaming milk into one of the cups. She watched as the girls added a spoon of sugar to this mixture and then proceeded to drink it.

'Yuck! What is this thing?' she asked, looking green.

'Egg flip,' grinned Seema, 'You gotta have one every morning.'

'But . . . but it's raw egg!'

'Makes you strong!' piped up Gayathri.

Shagun yelled for everyone to quickly finish their egg flips and get down to the bus. Noorie looked around and watched the girls downing the dreaded drink stoically. '*I can do this! I can do this!*' she thought. Arthi had finished hers and was now watching her, just like Seema and Gayathri.

She sniffed it and almost gagged at the foul smell. The others burst out laughing and even Arthi couldn't help smiling.

'Just pinch your nose and gulp it down, silly!' said Seema.

Noorie nodded and put on a brave face. She raised the cup to her lips with one hand, her nose pinched off by the other, and took a large sip. It tasted vile! It was the worst thing she had ever drunk! She swallowed it painfully, praying she wouldn't vomit.

'Just one more sip and you are done,' encouraged Gayathri.

Noorie looked around for water but couldn't find any. Her eyes were swimming with unshed tears. Arthi's smile had slipped a little now. She was watching Noorie with concern. The cup touched the lips again and the eggy milk filled Noorie's mouth but she couldn't bring herself to swallow it the second time, and before she knew it, she had spat it out on herself and the girls around her.

'Yuck!'

'Eeks!'

'You stupid idiot!'

'Now look what you've done!'

The girls yelled at her in disgust. She had soiled her brand-new track pants and she reeked of eggs. Shagun walked up and, seeing the scene, pursed her lips in anger.

'Go clean yourself up immediately! We have no time to waste. The rest of you get to the bus. *Now*!'

Shagun was mad. The first day of practice and this stupid girl had already made them late. Noorie sobbed quietly as she tried to wash off the egg flip from her jacket. At least it looked clean now, though the disgusting smell persisted.

'What a horrible start!' she thought miserably as she took her seat in the bus. Nobody wanted to sit near her as she stank, and Noorie looked morosely out of the window, barely registering the world around her.

'Do you realize this is the first time we have been out of the school since we got in?' asked Arthi as they got down at the training ground.

Noorie had been too busy feeling sorry for herself that she hadn't realized that. She widened her eyes and, for a moment, forgot her woeful state and smiled brightly.

'Even the air seems fresher and the birds chirp more happily outside the school,' she thought.

The two girls walked into the open-air stadium where their training would commence. The school owned this prestigious property but rented it out to others as well. The galleys were empty and the green oval in the centre glistened wetly. There were a few workers tidying up between the galleys. The rubberized track around the grass was a burnt orange in colour with clear white lines demarcating the tracks.

'This looks so hard-core,' whispered Noorie.

Arthi was in awe too. It was her first time too, and though Arthi tried not to show any interest, she couldn't help being impressed too.

'Looks good, doesn't it?' asked Seema, who had already changed into her shorts. 'I just wish I could spend all day on track rather than in that stuffy old classroom.'

Seema and books didn't really get along. She found it hard to follow, especially subjects like maths and science. But when it came to things like 100-metres, hurdles, or high jumps, she was full of zeal. She was like a gazelle on tracks, and Noorie and Arthi couldn't wait to see her in action.

Coach Rhonda was waiting for them in the oval and the girls quickly gathered around her. There were about fifty of them of varying ages and sizes. Noorie looked at some of the senior girls who towered over her. Their long legs seemed endless. They all looked trim, fit, and absolutely certain about what they were doing. Only she and Arthi looked out of place. Coach Rhonda quickly told them what they would be doing that day.

'Since it's the first day, we will take it easy. Just do three rounds of jogging on the 400-m track. We'll do some exercises after that and then we can do a few sprints and call it a day. We'll increase the pace over the week and then try out for various events next week, all right, girls?' she asked briskly.

The girls got on with it immediately with the seniors leading the way. The first round was quite all right for Noorie and Arthi, but halfway into the second round, both the girls were panting like dogs. They somehow managed to finish off the required three rounds and bent over exhausted as the rest of the girls made a large circle in the centre for exercises.

'Not something for weaklings now, is it?' sniggered Gayathri.

Arthi bristled but didn't have the energy to come up with a suitable retort. After a couple hundred jumping jacks, high knees, back kicks, squats, crunches, burpees, lunges, and other exercises that the new girls hadn't even heard about before they joined the seasoned athletes for sprints, they were divided into groups of five according to their ages, and Coach Rhonda and Ms Shobha stood at either end of a 100-meter track. Noorie watched the sun peeking over the mountains and struggling to shine through the dark cloud cover that refused to budge. Both she and Arthi watched the seniors whizz across the tracks, laughing as they reached the finish line. They looked so at home on the field. And when it was their turn to run, they fell far behind Seema, Gayathri, and a few other girls from class 6 and 8. Noorie's ears turned red in embarrassment, and she tried not to make eye contact with anybody. Meanwhile, Arthi couldn't care less.

'It's not like I'm an athlete anyway,' Arthi thought, her face set in a mutinous expression.

Coach Rhonda watched the new girls closely. She knew she couldn't expect miracles in a day but she hoped they would show the stuff they were made of.

'That was pathetic,' thought Noorie as she climbed into the bus. Her thighs and calves were sore and her whole body felt wobbly. She had come last consistently in all of her sprints and she was disgusted with herself. At the end of the last sprint, she had been close to throwing up from exhaustion. That nasty egg flip seemed to have worked its way up to her throat and threatened to erupt. She took deep gulps of cool mountain air to calm her churning stomach and looked outside at the dark green pines glistening with raindrops.

Arthi collected her belongings and slowly made her way to the bus. She had been better off than Noorie. After a few sprints, she had managed to outrun two others in her group and so her mood was quite light. She stood in line to board the bus; the girls in front of her joked and laughed. She looked around, taking stock of her surroundings. Ooty was slowly coming to life. The grey rain had lifted, and a pale July sun shone down upon them now. A few cars, buses, and autos navigated the twists and turns in the town. There was some sort of public school near the stadium, and Arthi watched parents dropping off their wards in scooters and cars. She watched a lady with a head of frizzy, curly hair bend down to kiss her little one and her heart clenched. She missed her mother so much suddenly. As the lady stood up and walked away, Arthi saw something that made her heart beat like a sledgehammer—*a big red postbox.* She whooped silently with joy. She had finally found a way to get a letter across to her mother. She just had to make sure she stayed on the sports team so she could make her way to the stadium and then she could post all the letters she wanted. The bigger problem now, however, was how she was going to get some envelopes and stamps. She frowned as she got into the bus and remained silent all the way to school, worrying about the next step in her plan.

Breakfast after sports practice was a spread fit for royalty. The girls had the dining hall all to themselves, and with no nuns to supervise them, they were in their element. They could pick their own places at the ten tables set out for them, and they sat next to their friends and classmates chatting nineteen to a dozen. Trays of soft, golden-yellow scrambled eggs, crispy strips of beef bacon, chicken sausages, tiny roasted baby potatoes, baked tomatoes, baked beans in tomato gravy, loaves of freshly baked white bread, and piles of butter balls had them gasping in pleasure. Huge jugs of freshly squeezed orange juice sat on each table. The athletes were ravenous, and it was obvious that the nuns firmly believed that full stomachs = happy athletes. The girls stuffed their faces and forgot their sore, aching muscles.

'Girls, hurry up and get clean, OK? I don't want any of you to reach class later than ten o'clock, got it?' yelled Shagun. 'No complaints from teachers about athletes being too late!'

By the time Noorie and the others reached class, the first period was over; they had just missed maths under Ms Sindhu's sharp eye.

'One of the other benefits of sports practice,' sniggered Seema.

The girls got busy with their lessons. They had a quiz during the geography lesson in which Noorie shone because geography was one of her favourite subjects and she had done a lot of extra reading on wind erosion. Her team was thrilled with her and she got quite a few pats and handshakes for her efforts. She gleamed with pleasure.

The girls waited anxiously for Ms Bartley and the marks for their latest science test. Meenu was boasting to Usha about how well she had done in hers.

'I knew all the questions. In fact, for a few of them I even wrote extra points, you know. I'm sure Ms Bartley will be pleased with me,' said Meenu, beaming.

Usha was not impressed. She didn't even like Meenu but only spent time with her because she helped her with her studies, especially science and maths. None of the other girls seemed to like her and she didn't really care. But Meenu was so full of her studies and books that she didn't mind Usha tagging along after her. Usha barely paid attention to anything she said except when she was tutoring her. And Meenu was thankful for Usha's company, for none of the other girls hung out with her. They found her too boring and made fun of her enormous black-framed glasses and boundless knowledge.

'A bunch of morons,' she thought as she glanced around her class.

'Good afternoon, girls,' said Ms Bartley as she walked in daintily like a bird. She waved the science test papers and asked the girls to take their seats. There was a hush in class as the girls sat down nervously.

'The marks of this test are very important as it covers all the topics we finished in the past few weeks. For those of you who have done badly, I will write a note which needs to be signed by your parents or, in the case of the boarders, by the boarding mistress,' she said and the class erupted into groans and protests.

'Silence!' she yelled, her eyes flashing.

'Now, Radhica, come forward and distribute the papers,' she said.

Radhica sprang from her seat and started distributing the papers as fast as she could. The faces of the girls reflected their performance. There were smiles, there were tears, and there were even a few shocked expressions. There were also a few indifferent ones and Ms Bartley scrutinized the class for those faces; one of them was Arthi's. She hadn't done very well as she hadn't prepared for it. She had known the test was a serious one but her worries about her mother and her continuous planning for getting a message out to her kept her mind constantly occupied. She had little interest in her lessons these days, and she was falling behind week after week.

'Ma'am, ma'am!' called out Meenu in a high voice disturbing Ms Bartley's observation routine.

'What is it, child?' she snapped.

'Ma'am, I think you didn't mark me right. I should have got one more mark for question 3, 6, and 8. I have written more points than the others,' she complained.

'Oh? *Have you?*' replied Ms Bartley. Her voice had taken on a slight sarcasm that was lost on Meenu.

Meenu thought she was being encouraged and so she bounded up to the teacher's table with a wide smile. The other girls stopped counting their marks, rereading their answers, and comparing papers with their neighbours. A pin-drop silence fell upon the class. They could hear the papers rustling as Ms Bartley glanced at the answers pointed out by Meenu.

'Go back to your seat now,' she instructed and Meenu went back, looking a little puzzled.

'Now, girls, this is an *example* for all of you,' Ms Bartley continued, and Meenu grinned from her seat. She couldn't believe Ms Bartley was so impressed by her work.

'Of what *not* to do!' yelled Ms Bartley.

Meenu blanched in shock. *What was she saying?* She had written everything the teacher had said in class and she had added extra points from the textbook and other reference books she had read in the library. She was certain her answers were the best ones in the class.

'When I ask you to write a definition, I only need *one* definition. I don't need *three*! And when ask you for three properties of metals, I want only *three* and not *five*! And when I say write *one* paragraph about non-metals, I expect six to seven lines and not an *entire* page mugged up from multiple textbooks!'

Ms Bartley was livid with rage. The girls cowered in fear, and Meenu was as white as a sheet.

'Now, I will show you a paper of what I expect. Noorie, come up here,' she yelled startling Noorie, who jumped up instinctively and handed over her paper.

'*This* is the way to write a test. *Precise*, and filled with only *necessary* information. *This* girl has prepared well. She has read my notes thoroughly and looked over the topic in the prescribed textbook. That's all you need to know. And she has followed my instructions to the letter Look at her paper and learn a lesson or two,' said Ms Bartley, looking straight at Meenu, who quailed under the sharp words.

Noorie sat back in her seat, in stunned silence.

'Well done!' whispered Radhica with a smile.

Noorie looked around and found a few more encouraging nods, smiles, and thumbs-up signs. She turned back to where Meenu sat and caught her hateful look. She was the class nerd and now there was a usurper in class and that too a new girl; Meenu was beside herself with rage. Usha looked at her and made a slashing motion with her fingers below her neck. Noorie gulped. *What had she gotten herself into?*

Arthi lay in bed that night plotting about finding letter paper. She thought of all the people who could leave school every day and who had access to money and the post office. That would be the teachers and the day scholars. Asking the teachers was out of question, so that left her with only one option: find a sympathetic day scholar. She sighed as she turned over. This was turning into a long drawn-out plan. She knew the names of the all the day scholars and had exchanged just inane pleasantries with them over the past few weeks, but she didn't know anyone well enough to ask a favour like this. How was she going to have a conversation with each one of them and find out where their sympathies lay? But her appa's face popped into her mind at that moment, and she shut her eyes tightly, willing it to go away. *She would find a way, she would!*

# Chapter 8

# THE POSTBOX

Sports practice continued without respite seven days a week. Arthi improved her running times, and Coach Rhonda smiled in approval. Noorie was still coming last in her batch but she had improved too. She was faster and her stamina was much better. In two weeks, the girls could feel the difference in their bodies. They were faster and stronger. Arthi continued to gaze longingly at the red postbox every morning, assuring herself she would be able to post a letter through it one day. In the meantime, she was taking baby steps in seeking out the day scholars. She made it a point to greet them every morning and tried to share a few laughs and jokes with them. But this was met with curious and suspicious stares. They never let her into their circle. She was an outsider, a boarder, someone they didn't trust or even like.

'Why do you keep trying to talk to dayskees?' asked Radhica one evening at tea.

'What do you mean?' replied Arthi, pretending the question didn't bother her.

'I mean, you've been sniffing around them all week. What's the deal? Don't you like us boarders? Is that why? Are you trying to find a friend among them because you can't find one here?' continued Radhica.

The other girls stopped eating and watched Arthi with interest. Radhica was asking a question they were all dying to ask. They had all noticed Arthi's overtures to the day scholars and had been curious about it.

'It's *none* of your business,' spat out Arthi angrily. She threw down her buttered toast and left the dining table in a huff.

'Oh dear!' mumbled Noorie.

'What? Was there something wrong in what I asked?' bristled Radhica. 'It's true, isn't it?'

'It *is* true, Radhica, but I don't think there was any need to corner her like that. And besides I really don't understand this whole *don't talk to the dayskees* thing. Just because some seniors started it doesn't mean we have to follow it blindly without reason or logic,' replied Noorie.

'*This* school was built on *tradition*. We follow the rules laid down for us by our teachers and just as importantly by our *seniors*. If they say *don't* do something, *we* don't do it. No questions asked. That's the way we are raised here,' replied Radhica. Her voice rose with every sentence, and the girls were staring at each other hotly.

'I think that's a load of crap,' said Noorie, and the girls at the table gasped.

'Did you just say our *traditions* are crap? Our *seniors* are crap?' yelled Radhica.

Noorie realized she had put her foot in her mouth but it was too late to back down. She didn't know what had gotten into her. She hadn't meant to offend anyone; she was just trying to understand. She pursed her lips shut and left the table, while the others booed and sniggered. Her ears burned and she walked off to the study hall to find Arthi. She knew Radhica and the other girls would be angry with her, and that meant she had to find at least one ally.

'Did I ask you to speak up for me? I can fight my own battles, thank you very much,' said Arthi to an open-mouthed Noorie.

Here she was thinking she could find one friend, and it turned out that even Arthi blamed her for her outburst. Her heart sank. She was fighting a battle that she didn't even really care enough about. Radhica, Jenna, and the other girls walked into the study hall, pointedly ignoring the two of them. Over the next hour, they refused to make eye contact or even respond to Noorie's questions. It was like they couldn't see her, like she didn't exist. A large lump formed in Noorie's throat and tears threatened to roll down her cheeks. She was being punished for her 'crap' comment. She tried to apologize but no one seemed to be listening. Arthi watched in disgust as Noorie grovelled, trying to get back into everyone's good books again. She wished the girl had more spunk and stood her ground.

Noorie consoled herself, saying that she could weather the storm and it would probably last a day or two. But how terribly mistaken she was. If there was one thing the girls at the Royal Academy did well, it was giving the cold shoulder. They wouldn't so much as look in her direction, morning, noon, or night. The only people who talked to her were her teachers, a few seniors, and the day scholars in her class. Even Arthi gave her a wide berth much to her disappointment. Noorie was in a fix. She didn't know what to do now. She was terribly lonely all the time, especially in the evenings at the boarding. At least during the day she had sports practice, where she made a few friends outside her class group and the day scholars were quite all right. They knew something was amiss, and when Noorie confided in one of them, they tried to be nice to her though they didn't really take her into their fold. Arthi watched all this in frustration. Here she was trying to make headway with the day scholars, but it was Noorie who seemed to be winning their trust. With no boarders on her side, she was in a no man's land, which suited the day scholars just fine.

After two weeks of the silent treatment, Radhica finally relented. She asked Noorie to apologize publicly to all the boarders in her class, which she did with relief. Though she had enjoyed her time with the day scholars, she missed her boarder friends much more.

'So does this mean you won't be talking to us anymore?' asked one of the day scholars, a girl called Myra, who was pretty, skinny, with long plaits.

'Of course not! It just means they've forgiven me. That's all. I enjoyed talking with you girls and you were all nice to me. Of course I am going to stay friends with you all, especially you, Myra,' replied Noorie.

'Hmm . . . let's see,' smiled Myra.

But Noorie was true to her word. She spent her afternoon break time with Myra and a few other girls in the *dayskee* gang. She didn't, however, try to convince

Radhica or the others of what she thought was an error in their ways.

'To each their own,' she thought, remembering something Sr. Molly said once during morning studies.

Arthi was running out of time. Her father had written to her, saying he might be coming down to visit her during the free weekend at midterm in August. She was dreading it. She waited in vain for letters and phone calls from her mother, who seemed to have fallen off the face of the earth. *Was she really being given away to her appa?* She was almost beside herself with anxiety on getting his letter. She could wait no longer. The free weekend was just two weeks away and she had to contact her mother. The friendship with day scholars didn't seem to be working out for her. But they all seemed quite taken by Noorie. So that left her with just one option—*ask Noorie for help.* She took a deep breath, swallowed her pride and doubt, and walked up to Noorie, who was reading a Nancy Drew book in the study hall.

'Hi!' said Arthi, shuffling her feet.

'Hi?' Noorie was surprised. She hadn't talked to Arthi in days.

'Can I talk to you?'

'You are now, aren't you?'

'Yeah, but privately.'

'OK. Where do you have in mind?'

'Back compound?'

'What? With all those little girls screaming on the swings and see-saws?'

Arthi nodded and Noorie laughed silently as she got to her feet.

But the back compound was quiet. The rain had kept the little ones indoors. Arthi and Noorie walked through the sodden grass. It was going to be dark soon, so Arthi had to be quick about it.

'I want to tell you about my family,' she began, taking a deep breath.

Arthi talked non-stop for about half an hour and Noorie listened attentively. Her sympathy and respect for Arthi grew as her story unfolded. Arthi didn't spare her any details. Once she started talking, she just couldn't stop. She had kept all those fears and worries locked up inside her chest for so long that now that it was a relief to talk to someone. She created a vivid picture of a home with two strong but fundamentally different adults tearing apart their family with their differences. She told her about her terror of being taken away by her father and his parents, how she believed they were trying to keep her mother away from her. And finally she confessed that she needed Noorie's help to put her plan in action.

'I hope you don't think I'm trying to take advantage of you and your friendship with the day scholars. But you understand now what a mess I'm in, don't you?' Arthi asked anxiously.

Noorie was quiet for a little while. She needed some time to absorb all that she had heard. Arthi's world was so different from her own.

'Can I think about it, please?' she asked softly.

Arthi's face fell. She knew Noorie was about to reject her request and she couldn't see any other options.

'I will help you. But I just need tonight to think about it, please,' reassured Noorie, squeezing Arthi's hand.

Arthi nodded vigorously. She was perilously close to tears of gratitude.

That night as Noorie lay in bed, listening to Arthi fall asleep, she felt her heart go out to her. Noorie thanked her lucky stars that her home looked boring compared to the drama in Arthi's. The worst thing her father did was boss them around and yell at her mom sometimes, but at least they loved each other and theirs was a happy home. He was kind and loving and took great care of all of them. She shuddered to think of what she would have done if her dad were like Arthi's appa. *What a scary man he was! And threatening one's own child! Horrid man!*

'OK! I'll do it,' she whispered to Arthi the next morning while they brushed their teeth, shoulder to shoulder.

Arthi squealed and hugged her with joy. Radhica and Jenna looked at them strangely.

'What were they up to now?' they thought, shaking their heads in exasperation at these two new girls.

Noorie's plan was to ask Myra for help, of course. Of all the day scholars, she liked Myra the most. She was also the most different from all of them. She explained Myra's situation to Arthi before morning studies.

Noorie waited for lunchtime to get hold of Myra. She had told Arthi that she would handle it alone. Myra didn't know or trust Arthi enough to help her.

'Psst! I have to talk to you,' whispered Noorie, grabbing Myra's hand urgently.

'Oookay!' said Myra, rolling her eyes at the hush-hush manner.

Arthi watched as the two girls left the classroom and walked in the front courtyard where other children were eating lunch, playing, and chatting. She was worried Myra would say no. After three rounds of the courtyard, Myra and Noorie made their way back to class. Noorie gave Arthi a smile and wink as she sat down for the next lesson. Arthi was so anxious that she had bitten off all her fingernails by the time all the classes were over.

'So? What did she say?' asked Arthi eagerly when she got Noorie alone for a moment in the Yellow Dorm.

'She said her dad keeps stamps and stationery in his study. She can get us an envelope and the necessary stamps tomorrow itself,' whispered Noorie, bursting with happiness.

'Thank you! Thank you! Thank you!' said Arthi, enveloping Noorie in a tight bear hug. 'I can't tell you how grateful I am! Thank you so, so much!'

# Chapter 9

# THE LETTER

It was a bright Sunday morning. The sun was shining and it looked like the rain would hold off today. Most of the girls were out in the playground enjoying this brief respite from the incessant rains that pounded on them the last few days. Only a few girls sat in the study hall, and Arthi was one of them. She was working on something.

Arthi read and reread her letter several times to make sure she had conveyed her message. She folded the letter paper and tucked it into her envelope. She couldn't find her glue stick and so she decided to leave it in her desk, hidden inside her science textbook. She sighed with relief and left to join Noorie and the others, who were playing volleyball.

Usha and Meenu were also in the study hall. Meenu was busy mugging up the periodic table as she was trying to get back into Ms Bartley's good books again. She didn't want Noorie to have the upper hand, and she believed Ms Bartley would be most impressed with her memory skills in the next lesson. Usha was knitting a muffler.

Usha wondered what Arthi was working on so intently at her desk on a bright and shiny Sunday morning when she could be outside with the others. Her curiosity got the better of her, and she went over to Arthi's desk. She quietly looked around her and saw that no one was paying any attention to her. She opened the desk and rummaged around. She didn't even know what she was looking for. Just then she noticed something blue peeking out from inside the science textbook.

'A letter? Hmmm . . . interesting,' she mumbled as she quietly sat down to read it.

> My dear Amma,
>
> I hope you are well. I am terribly worried about you as I haven't heard from you since long. Are you OK? Sr. Josephine said something about a fall. Are you in the hospital? Have you hurt yourself? I haven't received any letters or phone calls and I don't know what is happening to you in Madras. Why don't you call me anymore? Or write to me?
>
> Appa was here to visit me a few weeks ago. It was not a nice visit. He said some scary things. He said I would have to go to Tirunelveli to live with Thatha and

Patti and that I would not be allowed to live with you. Is this right? Is that why you are not writing to me or calling me? Are you going to let him have me, Amma?

I can't imagine that, Amma! It scares me every night. I know he is my appa but I really don't like him. I wish I never knew someone like him. I'm pretty sure he doesn't even love me for real. After his visit, I begged Sr. Josephine to let me call you. But she refused and sent me out of her room. Nasty nun!

They read all our letters here and so I couldn't write to you through the boarding either. This is letter is being sent through other secret ways, so that Sr. Nasty Nun cannot get her hands on it. (I don't want anyone to read my letters to you, Amma.) Also, I think she's impressed with Appa. She had a funny smile on her face when he came to visit. Silly nun! She is the only thing I don't really like about this school otherwise everything is quite OK.

Please, Amma! Do reply to my letter as soon as you receive it. Will you come to visit me for the free weekend on Aug 14th? Please, please, please! I am dying to

see you. I love you so much and I miss
you like crazy, my dear, sweet Amma!

With all my love,
Arthi.

Usha put back the letter exactly where she found it.
She then went back to her seat and sat down quietly lost
in thought. *How did she get the letter paper and stamps?
And how is she planning to post it without Sr. Josephine
knowing about it?*

Usha's interest was piqued. She decided to observe
Arthi and find out more. Usha was really good at
observing others. She was a great Sherlock Holmes fan
and believed a lot could be learnt about others by just
observing them. She had noticed the sudden warmth
between Arthi and Noorie over the last few days.
Something had changed in their relationship. *Maybe
Noorie is helping her.* If she could find out more about
the plan, then she could get them both in trouble. She
hugged herself with glee. She loved making trouble for
others. It was so much fun to sit on the sidelines and
watch someone else get mauled by Sr. Josephine. And
besides she was angry that Radhica and the other old
girls were so quick to accept Arthi and Noorie into their
gang. They had never included Usha and now she would
make those smug new girls pay. She giggled aloud,
thinking of what fun lay ahead for her. Meenu looked
at her in annoyance as her giggles had distracted her.

'The letter is ready,' said Arthi to Noorie after lunch.
'Good! Good! So we take it to sports practice and
post it. That's our plan, right?'

Arthi nodded happily.

'I hope nothing goes wrong,' said Noorie.

'What could possibly go wrong? We have the envelope and stamps and we have access to a post box. It will all go like clockwork,' replied Arthi.

'Fingers crossed!'

'Come on, let's go listen to some Madonna in the play room. One of the seniors bought a new cassette and the songs are fab,' replied Arthi.

Both Arthi and Noorie were quite used to the ugly taste of egg flip now. They slugged it back like the rest of the athletes and Noorie didn't even gag the last few times. She was quite proud of herself for that. Arthi was doing really well at practice and Coach Rhonda had moved her to the top set with Seema and Gayathri to challenge her further and improve her times. Noorie, meanwhile, laboured in the substitutes batch. She hoped she wouldn't be taken off the team as she was quite enjoying the routine and the breakfast was a huge plus.

The girls were off to the stadium as usual in school bus. Prem Anna, the driver, had brought a new audio cassette and the bus was filled with the latest tunes from some Rajnikant movie. Prem Anna was a big fan of his and the only songs the girls could listen to in his bus were those from his movies. But they didn't mind. Their entertainment options were limited and so anything was welcome.

'So, today is D-day,' whispered Noorie.

Arthi nodded. She was a little tense. Her cocksure confidence was not where it was yesterday. She prayed nothing would go wrong.

Sports practice went on as routine. Arthi was a little distracted and was pulled up by Coach Rhonda a few times.

'Are you not well, Arthi?' she asked.

'No, no, Coach. I'm fine!' Arthi replied

'Well, you seem a little under the weather. Is everything all right?'

'Yes, yes!'

And Arthi ran to join the others in her batch. After practice the girls started collecting their spikes and other equipment they had brought along for the training session. The seniors always boarded the bus first and the juniors followed as per seniority. Arthi's classmates were always the last ones to board, followed by the coach. She watched as girls laughed and chatted as they made their way to the bus. She just needed a minute to run to the post box and drop off her letter. Just one minute of privacy where no one would see what she was doing. Arthi nodded to Noorie, who was taut with tension.

'Go!' mouthed Noorie silently.

Arthi ran towards the postbox, praying no one was looking in her direction. Noorie's eyes darted back and forth, looking at Arthi's progress and at the crowd near the bus.

'Hey! Isn't that one of our girls?' shouted Coach Rhonda suddenly.

'Shit! Shit!' cursed Noorie.

Coach Rhonda, who was speaking to Ms Shobha about the nearby school, had suddenly turned around to show her something. And that's when she saw a little girl in her blue-and-white tracksuit racing away from the bus.

'Hey! Stop!' she yelled and broke into a run.

Noorie watched in horror as she gained speed and closed the distance. The other athletes had stopped talking, and they were all watching in amazement as Coach Rhonda zipped through the crowds and caught Arthi just as she reached the post box.

'Wow! Who knew Coach could run so fast?' One of the girls whistled.

'Who is that kid? One of the juniors, right?'

The seniors were looking down now at Noorie, Seema, and Gayathri, who were squirming in embarrassment.

'Your classmate, right? What's her name? And where did she think she was running off to? Moron!'

The juniors didn't say a word. They just stood like statues near the bus as they watched a weeping Arthi being dragged back by an irate Coach Rhonda.

'What the hell was she doing?' whispered Seema.

Noorie shrugged. She didn't want to give out any information. She prayed Arthi had been able to post that damn letter. Otherwise it was all for nothing! She couldn't see from where she stood if the letter was still in Arthi's hand. Her heart sank after a few minutes when she saw the envelope clutched in Coach Rhonda's hands.

'Get into the bus! Now! All of you!' yelled Coach Rhonda.

Her face was red with anger and exertion. She was furious. The girls were her responsibility when they were outside the school premises. In all her years coaching, not one child had tried something stupid like. *What if a bus had hit her? Or someone had kidnapped her?* Coach thanked all the gods for the lucky escape.

Arthi was sobbing incessantly during the entire ride back home. She wasn't allowed to sit with Noorie or the others. Coach Rhonda kept her close by, almost as if she expected Arthi to leap out of the bus or do something equally stupid and dangerous. Arthi couldn't believe her bad luck. *If only she had been just a few seconds faster, she would have made it! Why did Coach Rhonda have to see her? Why couldn't God help her just this once?* She was angry and upset and sorry for herself all at once.

Noorie sat alone in the bus. She was just as worried as Arthi. She knew that the nuns would now question Arthi and try to find out how she got the stamps and envelope. *Would Arthi spill the beans? What if she mentioned Myra's name and hers? What punishment would they get? What if Arthi was expelled? What if she was expelled? What if they only expelled Myra because she was the one who got the stamps for them? How would she live with the guilt?* Noorie was terrified of all the different scenarios that kept playing in her head.

'Shagun, take her for breakfast, get her changed, and then bring her directly to Sr. Josephine's office,' instructed Coach Rhonda.

She had calmed down and she looked as if she had made up her mind about what needed to be done. Shagun grabbed Arthi's hand and took her along. Breakfast that day was a quiet affair for the juniors.

'Did you know about this?' asked Seema.

Noorie didn't say anything. She chewed her idlis with intense concentration.

'Of course she did!' spat out Gayathri. 'The two are best buds, aren't they?'

'What was she trying to do? Run away? That's not even the direction of the bus station. What an ass,' mumbled Seema.

Both the girls were cross with Arthi for showing them in bad light in front of the others. And since she wasn't around, Noorie got Arthi's share of insults. But she kept her mouth shut. She didn't want to give away anything. She didn't know how it would all pan out in the end. She had to watch and wait and that was the terrible part—the waiting. She looked over to where Arthi sat, near Shagun at the seniors' table. She looked broken, eyes down and face still puffy after all her crying.

'What a pity,' thought Noorie. 'She is worse off now.'

Coach Rhonda waited outside Sr. Josephine's office with a silent Arthi. The letter was still in her hand.

'You were trying to post the letter, weren't you? But why? Don't you girls write home every week?' she asked.

Arthi didn't say anything.

'Aren't you happy here, Arthi? What's going on with you, girl? If you tell me, maybe I can help you,' urged Coach Rhonda, feeling a twinge of guilt.

'You are all the same. You are all with him,' mumbled Arthi, looking straight into Coach Rhonda's eyes.

'Him?' Coach was puzzled. *What was this girl talking about?*

Arthi kept her mouth shut and looked at her feet mutinously.

Sr. Josephine called for them to enter the office. She was in a cheery mood.

'Good morning, Sister,' said Coach Rhonda.

'Good morning, Rhonda. I haven't seen you in a while. How are the girls doing? Practice is going well, I hope. And the athletes this year, how are they? Any chance of a first place this time?' She smiled.

'Umm . . . yes . . . yes. It's all going quite well, Sister. Actually I'm here because of something that happened this morning at the stadium,' Coach Rhonda began uneasily.

'Oh? And what is that?' enquired Sr. Josephine. The smile had vanished from her face and she was looking very serious now.

Coach Rhonda narrated the incident with as little emotion as possible. She didn't try to embellish or exaggerate. She just said it as it had happened. Sr. Josephine watched her like a hawk throughout the whole story and took her eyes off her face only in the end, to stare at Arthi. The room was ominously quiet after Coach Rhonda stopped her narration. Sr. Josephine sat back in her high chair; she hadn't even realized that she had moved forward to the edge of her seat as the story had proceeded. *This was a very serious incident. The foolish child couldn't have hurt herself running through the traffic and crowds like that.*

'Hand me the letter,' she said with an eerily calm voice.

Coach Rhonda glanced once at Arthi with regret and then handed over the letter to Sr. Josephine. She pried it open with her shiny silver letter opener. The silence in the room made Arthi breathless as she watched her words tumbling out of the letter.

'How dare you? How dare you?' said Sr. Josephine, rising from her chair, quivering with anger.

She towered over Arthi, who shrank back in her seat. Sr. Josephine was shaking with anger and she was waving the letter like a maniac. Her eyes were like slits, and flecks of saliva landed on Arthi, Coach, and the table as she yelled abuses.

*'Oh dear God! I have unleashed a monster!'* thought Arthi.

'It's children like you who give a bad name to schools like ours. Badly raised by incompetent parents and bringing your troubles into this esteemed school. With ill-matched parents like yours and with the kind of upbringing you have had, I shouldn't be surprised at your antics! You think your mother is some kind of saint?' she ranted. 'Well, she isn't! Your father has told me all about her character and about her many shortcomings. If she had been a better person, then you would at least have a chance at being something. Your father is just trying to save you from your evil mother's influence. But then the devil is always more attractive, isn't it? And it looks like you are just like her!'

Coach Rhonda was shocked by the viciousness of the attack on Arthi. She had no idea what the contents of the letter were, but she could see that the situation was spinning out of control. Clearly, Sr. Josephine was losing her mind in her anger.

'Sister! Umm . . . Sister, perhaps we should take a moment to calm ourselves down,' she suggested.

'Calm down! Are you serious, Rhonda? Parents send their useless children to us to fix them, to make them right, to make them normal, fit to live a normal life. But some of them are just damaged goods. And spending time and energy on them is just worthless!'

Coach Rhonda gasped at the language the nun was using.

'Sister, please! This is a simple matter that can be resolved with some small punishment. She wasn't trying to run away. She was only trying to post a letter!'

'A simple matter? Of course not! The rot runs deeper than you can see, Rhonda.'

'Sister, I think Arthi needs to get back to class now. Perhaps we can discuss this later,' suggested Coach Rhonda, trying to resolve the crisis.

Sr. Josephine opened her mouth to say something more, but just then, the telephone rang. She took a few seconds to rein in her temper and calm herself down and then picked up the receiver. Coach Rhonda and Arthi quietly slipped away.

They stood outside the office for a moment, both of them stunned by the verbal assault on Arthi. Coach almost regretted the whole incident. She could see that she just made matters worse for Arthi.

'The child was only trying to post a letter to her mother, for God's sake! It's not as if she was writing to a boyfriend or worse. A simple scolding and punishment would have been more than enough. There was surely no need for all those ugly words and nasty comments about the child's mother and her character,' she thought sadly as she looked at the crumpled form of Arthi.

'Arthi, you need to get to class now. I don't want you to believe anything Sr. Josephine said today, all right?' she asked, grasping Arthi's shoulders and willing her to look into her eyes.

What she saw tore at her heart. The child was in so much pain, and her eyes were bright with unshed tears. Clearly she had a troubled family, or at least that was what Sr. Josephine had said. Coach felt sorry for all that Arthi had to see and endure in so short a time.

'You are a good, sweet child. You wanted to write to your mother and you wanted to let her know something personal, I understand that. But what you did today was dangerous. Do you realize that?' continued Coach kindly.

Arthi nodded half-heartedly.

'I just wanted to let her know I'm scared,' she whispered.

Coach wanted to hug the poor girl and tell her all would be well, but she didn't know if it was the right thing to do. She wished she had never caught her running to the post box in the first place.

'Go to class now. This will all die down in a few days. See you at practice tomorrow,' Coach said as she walked to the staff room with a heavy heart.

Things got worse as the week progressed. Ms Rani was told about the incident and she gave Arthi an earful for her antics. Arthi withdrew into a shell and refused to speak about it to anyone. The only person who could still reach out to her was Noorie, who was very concerned for her friend's well-being. Radhica, Jenna, and the others tried to get information out of Noorie but in vain. Arthi got her due punishment from Sr. Josephine. She was to do without her weekly tuck shop visits and couldn't see the weekly movie the girls saw every Sunday. This made her days bleaker. Noorie shared her candy and chips with her and tried to take her mind off the whole thing, but Arthi was locked in a little box of misery that she just couldn't get out of.

Meanwhile, Ms Rani was on the lookout for the person who supplied the stamps. She guessed that it must be one of the day scholars, though they didn't have a precedent for helping the boarders. She had no idea where to look. None of the day scholars seemed sympathetic or friendly with Arthi in particular. The pressure was mounting on her to find the culprit and she was quite at her wits' end.

One morning she found an anonymous note inside the attendance register. Whoever had placed it there knew she would be the first person to read it, as it was her lesson which was the first one that day. She looked around in the class, trying to find the owner of the note but couldn't really make out. She didn't catch Usha's sly smile behind her textbook. Ms Rani read the note again.

*Noorie + Myra = Stamps.*

That was all the note said. And that was all Ms Rani needed.

By that evening, both the girls had confessed to their hand in the plan, and an outraged Ms Rani sent them packing to meet the principal. The two girls stood quivering in fear outside the principal's office. Her secretary, Mrs Poornima, a kind woman, tried to ease their fears.

'Just apologize for whatever you have done. Don't back answer. She hates it. Just listen to what Sister has to say and take your punishment meekly,' she advised the terrified girls.

The seniors called Sr. Rosemary the Nazi. She had a fearsome reputation and nobody messed with her. Her tongue was vicious, and errant girls were often given a verbal lashing they would remember for life. The worst thing that could happen to anyone was being called to the Nazi's office. Noorie had never expected herself to land up in a situation like this. She was never a rule-breaker and she had never found herself in a situation like this previously. Sr. Rosemary rang a bell from inside, and Mrs Poornima ushered the reluctant girls in.

Noorie stepped into the room and was immediately struck by how different it was from Sr. Josephine's office.

'Well, well, well,' Sr. Rosemary began speaking in a soft, raspy voice, 'what do we have here? A couple of Good Samaritans?'

The girls were numb with fear.

'Do you have anything to add?' she asked, looking at them, ominously raising her near-invisible eyebrows.

The girls shook their heads, not trusting themselves to speak.

Sr. Rosemary launched into a tirade about the lack of discipline and honesty in a school as fine as this one. And she spoke of how this disease was spreading among the girls and that it needed to be stopped.

'It's like a forest fire. Hard to get control of once it gets started. You start lying, cheating, and sneaking things for yourself, your friends. And before you know it, it becomes a nasty bad habit you cannot shake off.'

'Myra, bring your father to see me tomorrow. I will have a word with him about what his precious daughter is up to. And you, Noorie, since you are a boarder, I will let Sr. Josephine do what is needed to keep you in line. Now get out of my office and stay out of trouble. If I hear so much as a whisper about you girls again, you will be expelled!' she said, waving her finger threateningly.

The girls fell over themselves getting out of the office.

'I'm glad it's over,' said Noorie.

'For *you*, perhaps. I still have to bring my dad and it will be bad, I'm sure,' said Myra, looking downcast.

'I'm sorry I got you into this whole mess,' said Noorie.

'Well, it's too late now, isn't it?' replied Myra as they walked back to class.

'So are we still friends or what?' asked Noorie.

'Of course we are!' said Myra with a little smile on her pale face.

Noorie gave a deep sigh of relief. At least the gods had not abandoned her just yet.

# Chapter 10

# MIDTERM BREAK

'It's the free weekend! Yippee!' yelled Savita in the Yellow Dorm.

The girls were just waking up on Friday morning and already there was excited buzz in the air. Most of them would be going home or to nearby hotels with their parents, grandparents, or guardians for the free weekend. Noorie hoped her parents would drive up from Calicut. She was dying to see them. Arthi sat morosely in bed.

'Do you think your mom will come, Arthi?' asked Noorie.

Arthi shrugged. Lately she hardly spoke to anyone. She was sad and moody all the time. The only time she seemed happy was when she was out in the open, training in the stadium. But even there, she just did what was asked of her and never struck up a conversation or joined their fun and jokes. Coach Rhonda was concerned about her and had spoken to both Arthi and Noorie several times, trying to cheer the poor girl up.

The boarders were so excited about their parents coming down that most of them got into trouble in class.

'If I find you distracted one more time, Sreedevi, I will make you kneel down in that corner there!' threatened an exasperated Ms Sindhu.

Sreedevi couldn't imagine getting down on her pretty knees and kneeling in front of everyone and so she behaved for the rest of the lesson. She couldn't wait to see her grandmother. They had planned to stay at their guesthouse in Coonoor. No amount of threats and punishments could sink the buoyant moods of the girls. The lucky ones would be seeing their folks after two months, and they just couldn't stop smiling and building castles in the air.

'You have to try the chilli chicken and noodles at Shinkows,' yelled Jenna. 'It's simply divine! They make the best Chinese food in Ooty!'

'Don't forget to try the frankies at Archies. It's this kind of chapatti roll with an amazing chicken filling,' added Seema. 'My parents always take me there.'

'And if you want to buy books, go to Higginbothams. It's just opposite Chellaram's, the department store. Oh! By the way, Chellaram's has everything you could possibly need! It's huge!' said Radhica.

'Don't forget to pick up some home-made chocolates from Mohan's girls!' reminded Savita.

Noorie couldn't wait for class to be over. When the bell rang at 4.30 p.m., a whoop went up in the air, and the boarders streamed out of their classrooms and rushed to the front courtyard that was packed with cars and jeeps. Arthi stood near one of the railings, trying to see if her mother was anywhere around but she didn't see anyone resembling her and so she made her way quietly to the Yellow Dorm. She prayed her appa wouldn't come. Noorie was standing near the stone steps near Sr. Josephine's office, hoping and praying her parents would come and she squealed with glee when she saw the familiar car roll in through the boulevard. She flew down the steps and ran all the way to the car and hugged her mother before she had even stepped out.

'You came! You came!' she said over and over again.

'Of course, darling!' her mother replied.

'Where's Papa?' she asked, peering into the car, which was empty except for the driver.

'Oh! He had work, sweetie. He couldn't come. But we can phone him from the hotel, OK?' said her mother.

'OK,' said Noorie, a little sad. She had wanted to see her papa too. She missed his gigantic presence.

They quickly made their way to Sr. Josephine's office, and Noorie's heart stopped for a moment when she realized her mother would hear of her misdemeanours in a few minutes. In her excitement at meeting her parents, she had quite forgotten about the recent events.

'Mummy, there's something I need to tell you,' she began warily as they climbed the steps to the office.

She narrated the whole incident to her mother, not leaving out a single detail. She didn't dare look at her mother's face as she spoke for she was so ashamed of letting her down.

'Look at me, Noorie,' her mother said once she heard it all. Noorie looked up to find her mother smiling gently. Her eyes were a little moist too.

'Where is Arthi?' she asked.

'In the dorm, I think, Mummy. Why?' she replied, a little confused. She had thought her mother would be cross with her.

'Take me to her now,' she said, and a very surprised Noorie led her mother to the Yellow Dorm.

Arthi was standing by the window looking out into the courtyard, watching the parents roll in. She could hear muffled screams and laughs as girls met their parents. She saw a few hugs and kisses through the window, and she missed her mother terribly.

'Arthi!' called out Noorie from behind.

Arthi turned around to find Noorie and her mother. Her manners kicked in, in spite of her misery and she walked over to them quickly with a small smile, trying to hide her pain.

'Hello, Aunty,' she said softly, raising her hand for a handshake.

'Hello, dear!' replied Noorie's mother, taking in the little girl struggling with her worry and sorrow. She took a few steps forward and pulled her into her arms and hugged her gently.

'It's lovely to finally meet you, sweetie. Noorie has told me so much about you,' she said.

Both Noorie and Arthi were surprised by the sudden display of emotion, but they were both secretly pleased too. Arthi liked Noorie's mother instantly. She seemed warm and kind.

'Now, Noorie has told me all about your situation. So I need you to give me your Mummy's phone number so I can call and update her. Also you can write a letter to her if you wish and I will post it for you on Sunday when I take my leave. Is that fine, dear?' she asked.

Arthi nodded, tears of relief streaming down her cheeks. She hugged Noorie's mother once more and thanked her. A ray of hope seemed to pierce the dark cloud hanging over Arthi. A loud sob of relief escaped her.

'Ah! Shush now! It's the least I can do. If I could take you out with Noorie, I would have done it! Now tell me what you like to eat and we will get it for you tomorrow and we can have a little picnic somewhere inside school itself,' she suggested.

Noorie was open-mouthed with wonder. She had never seen her mother take so much initiative before. Back home, it was her father who decided and planned everything. Her mother just followed his instructions to a T. And here she was surprising her with her kindness to her friend, and her idea of the picnic was fantastic!

'I'm fine with anything, really. You don't have to trouble yourself, Aunty,' said Arthi, turning red with pleasure.

'She likes Chinese, Mummy,' said Noorie, smiling from ear to ear.

'Ah! Is it? Then we shall get some Chinese from the best restaurant in town. We will have a picnic lunch tomorrow, say, around two o'clock? OK? So don't eat too much from the school.' She winked at a laughing Arthi.

The meeting with Sr. Josephine was cold and angry. Sr. Josephine launched her assault on Noorie, who shrank in shame in her seat. But her mother sat up straighter and looked Sr. Josephine in the eye.

'Sister, I understand my daughter has made a mistake. But she is a *child*, please don't forget that. She has apologized and she has promised me that she won't do anything like this again. She is a good student and she will work hard and stay on the right track from now on. I think we can let the matter rest now. Thank you.' And with that, her mother stood up and pulled Noorie to the exit. She had dismissed the nun before she could be dismissed.

Sr. Josephine opened her mouth to respond, but by then, they had already left. She closed it again and mumbled something about uncultured parents breeding uncultured children and rang the bell impatiently to meet the next family.

Noorie and her mother stayed at Hotel Lakeview, in a quaint little cottage. The red-roofed cottage had one bedroom, an attached bathroom, a kitchenette, and a sitting-cum-dining room. A red coir carpet ran from wall to wall and the heater in the corner kept the room warm and toasty. Noorie talked and talked and talked. She had so much to say about the boarding, the school, her classes, teachers, friends, sports practice, the food, and so on. Her chatter was endless, and her mother laughed to see her daughter so happy. She didn't have to ask her to know that she had settled in well and was enjoying herself. Her grades were good too, and she was trying her hand at athletics and that was new for her. All in all, her mother was very pleased at how she was shaping up.

Her mother had packed her favourite snacks from home. Chicken samosas, beef cutlets, teardrop-shaped unnakkas (a sweet made from ripe bananas, with a coconut filling), banana halwa, yam chips, spicy tapioca chips, and more. Noorie ate like she hadn't eaten for a month, and her mother laughed to see her little glutton at work. The pair spent the whole evening in the cottage just eating and talking to their hearts' content.

Saturday morning was bright and shiny. There wasn't a single cloud in the baby-blue sky and Noorie thanked God for his mercy. They roamed around in the charming little town. They popped into Chellaram's to pick up a few toiletries, snacks, and some stationery for Noorie. An hour was spent in Higginbothams, browsing books. Both mother and daughter were avid readers. They left with bags of new Enid Blyton and Nancy Drew storybooks. It was nearing lunchtime, so they made their way to Shinkows and ordered the famous chilli chicken and noodles and made their way back to school.

Arthi was waiting for them with a big smile in the front courtyard, and the girls picked a quiet spot in the back compound that was practically deserted. Thankfully, the ground was not too wet.

'This is by far the best Chinese I have ever eaten! Thank you so much, Aunty!' pronounced Arthi in between little burps.

The girls lay sprawled in the grass while Noorie's mother cleared up the paper plates and leftovers. It was almost three o'clock and they stood up to leave.

'This is my mother's number, Aunty. Please call her and let her know what has happened. And please ask her to write to me. I don't understand why she doesn't,' said Arthi seriously.

Noorie's mother promised to call her right away and then get back to her at the earliest. Arthi stood in the corridor, watching them leave. She hoped they would be able to reach her mother finally.

Arthi's mother picked up her phone on the third ring. After the introduction, Noorie's mother told her all that had happened. She was horrified to learn that Arthi's mother was writing to her every week but it looked like someone was not giving her the letters!

'It must be that boarding mistress!' said Noorie's mother angrily.

'That nasty woman! I'm coming to school tomorrow itself,' replied Arthi's mother. 'I can be there by evening only. It's a long drive from here.'

'Good! We will wait for you then. We shall go and meet the nun together,' replied Noorie's mother.

She put down the receiver and sat quietly thinking about what she had heard. It looked like the boarding mistress was in cahoots with Arthi's father. She had been intercepting Arthi's mail and leading her to think her mother had abandoned her.

'What on earth was she thinking? How dare she try to pull off something like that? If someone did something like that to me, I would rip him or her apart! And the agony she made that poor child endure? It's criminal! It's shameful!' thought Noorie's mother. She was glad she was able to do something to resolve the matter.

The boarding mistress's office was the scene of a major drama on late Sunday evening. Raised voices could be heard outside, and other families outside wondered what was going on.

'Don't think you will get away with this, Sister,' warned Arthi's mother.

Her eyes were glinting with anger even though her face was lined and tired. She travelled a long way that day and was terribly exhausted, but she was trembling with fury just then.

'I will be complaining about you to the principal, the Mother Superior *here*, and your seniors in the Bishop's House,' she continued.

Sr. Josephine looked like an angry, wild animal. Her veil was askew and her face was purple with anger. She tried to argue but even she knew she had done the wrong thing. It was just her pride that didn't allow her to accept her mistake and apologize. Arthi's mother left, warning the nun not to try anything funny with her child once she left. Mother and daughter only had a few hours to spend together but Arthi didn't mind. She was radiant once more. Just seeing her mother was like balm to her wounded soul. She healed after weeks of pain and confusion. She was a strong, resilient child who had been badly shaken.

'I don't want you thinking about this anymore. There is nothing for you to worry about. The divorce is happening, and I have you for life, not your appa. Now all I want you to do is just study hard and play even harder. Promise?' said Arthi's mother just before she left for Madras.

'Yes, Amma!' smiled Arthi.

'Good! Now go kick some ass at that sports competition you have next month!' she said as a parting shot just before the car roared off.

Arthi laughed at her mother's language. She talked like one of *them*, not like a stuffy old parent. She was like a *friend* more than a parent and she loved her to bits.

# Chapter 11

# INTER-SCHOOL SPORTS

The day of the inter-school sports event loomed nearer and nearer. The athletes and Coach Rhonda were in a frenzy of last-minute preparations. Ms Shobha and Coach were also busy with deciding who would compete for the various sporting events in each category. The athletes were divided into five categories according to their ages—Sub-juniors, Juniors, Inters, Seniors, and Super-seniors. Typically children of class 5 were Sub-juniors, class 6 and 7 were Juniors, a few of class 7 and 8 were Inters, a few of class 8 and 9 were Seniors, and class 9 and 10 were Super-seniors. Arthi, Noorie, Seema, and Gayathri were in the Juniors category, and so were a few other girls from class 6. Both Arthi and Noorie were the substitutes for the main athletes in their category. They would have to step in only in case of injury, exhaustion, or illness. Noorie was quite all right with that, but Arthi was disappointed.

She had been training quite hard in spite of all her personal drama and she had really hoped she would get a chance to compete at the inter-school level. She was just a few seconds behind Seema every time, and she wished that she could give herself that final push.

'Don't worry, Arthi. There is always next year. And besides, since you are a few months younger than the others, you will still be Junior next year also while the other girls will be Inters. So you will have a better shot at it next year,' said Coach Rhonda.

But Arthi still felt heavy in the heart though she tried to put on a brave face and encourage the other girls. Noorie felt deeply for her. *If anyone deserved a break, it was Arthi*, she thought.

The inter-school sports event went on for two days. Day 1 was the *heats* that comprised the qualifying rounds for all events, including sprints, jumps, throws. Most schools sent at least two athletes per event to the qualifiers. Only the 4×100-m relay was excluded. Day 2 would have the final rounds for all events. Those who made it through the heats would be the finalists. Almost the entire boarding turned out in the front courtyard to wish their team luck. It was still early and most of them had just finished breakfast and morning studies were yet to start.

'Good luck, girls!'

'Do us proud!'

'You can do it!'

'Believe in yourself!'

The calls and cheers rang out in the courtyard. The athletes wore dark-brown cotton shirts and skirts. They wore their shorts underneath and most of them had their brown blazers on. The seal and motto of the school was embroidered on the pocket in bright yellow. Most of them were on the bus, while a few others were just joining them with their sports kits. The juniors were already seated and they were enjoying the attention. Even Sr. Josephine and Sr. Rosemary were out there, smiling and talking to the girls. Sr. Molly was on the bus, kissing the girls good luck and giving them hugs of cheer.

'I feel like a big-ass piece of chocolate!' laughed Arthi.

Shagun heard the comment and gave her a stern stare. The seniors didn't take too kindly to such remarks.

'Oops! I think she heard it,' giggled Noorie, who was beside her.

Arthi looked a little contrite. She felt the seniors were a little too stuck-up sometimes and this whole thing about traditions and respecting the past etc. etc. just went over her head.

'They could really do with a make-over,' she thought, looking down at their stuffy sports uniforms. 'I think our blue tracksuits looked way smarter. This makes us look *frumpy* like the old women!' But she held her tongue. She didn't anything to ruin this day as she was really looking forward to it.

Both the girls had heard a lot about the amazing MRC grounds where the sports extravaganza would be held at and they were yearning to see it. They were also curious to see the other schools that would turn out at the event. Seema and Gayathri had already filled them in about the various school colours and their sporting prowess.

'Now, St Joseph's has great athletes, both boys and girls. But none of them speak decent English,' Seema had said one day. 'It's more like a sports academy than a regular school. And they don't pay much attention to their studies. At least that's what one of the girls told me last year. Both the boys and the girls do really well at their sports events. Usually, St Joseph's is first among both girls and boys!'

'Watch out for Hills Academy. Those girls play real nasty. They'll try to elbow you and trip you and whatnot, but they manage to escape getting disqualified. Remember Coach Rhonda said something about it last year?' Gayathri had warned them.

So Arthi and Noorie knew a little bit here and there. St George's School wore gaudy golden-yellow sports uniforms but their athletes ran like the wind. The James Lawrence School kids looked menacing in their all-white uniforms but rarely performed well in the events. Nilgiris High School was a fancy school that rich kids went to and they just attended the event for fun. Their athletes were fat, untrained, and almost always came last. There was even a school in Coonoor with European kids, and their team had more white kids than brown. Noorie and Arthi wondered how good they would be this year.

The bus was on its way to the MRC grounds located at Wellington, which was an hour's drive away from the school. On the way, they passed the gorgeous Ketti Valley and marvelled at the enormous green valley that lay surrounded by lush, verdant Nilgiri hills. They were quite high up and so most of the houses in the valley looked like cute miniatures and the vehicles like colourful ants. While some of the land in the valley was still forested, large parts of it had been cleared for cultivation. It looked like a patchwork quilt of myriad shades of green. Noorie noticed that even some of the hills were being farmed. They looked like enormous steps on the hills with different crops on them. Noorie knew from Myra that a lot of vegetables like carrots, potatoes, cabbages, lettuce were grown in such terrace plantations.

'Look! Look! The lucky grotto is just around the corner. Girls, get ready with your wishes,' yelled one of seniors from up front.

The girls quickly sat upright in their seats, hoping for a glimpse of the lucky grotto. Noorie and Arthi knew all about it from Seema, of course. The lucky grotto was a very old shrine that was carved into the mountain by someone long ago. There was a statue of the holy Mother Mary in her blue-and-white garb, and people from all over Nilgiris came to pray here as they believed their prayers were always answered. The older girls swore by the grotto and said it always worked. Arthi was quite sceptical about the whole thing though. But Noorie was a fervent believer in luck and charms. Why, she even had a lucky pen that she wrote all her tests with, and she swore that was the reason she was doing well in class. Arthi had sniggered at all this mumbo-jumbo but today she kept silent.

The girls nearly missed the grotto, for Prem Anna, the driver, had decided at that very moment to overtake another school bus. There were shouts and groans as some of them missed it, while those who did manage to lock eyes with Mother Mary grinned triumphantly, certain they now had a direct line to the Almighty.

'What did you wish for?' asked Arthi.

Noorie's eyes were still closed, and her lips were moving fervently even though they were a few hairpin bends away from the grotto.

'Shh! Don't disturb me! I'm trying to pray!' she whispered, with closed eyes.

Arthi snorted with muffled laughter and sat back quietly in her seat and looked outside. They had already passed the town of Coonoor, with its colonial buildings and railway station set between tall pines and eucalyptus trees. Someone had pointed out St Joseph's School that stood atop a hill glaring down at passersby.

'Girls! We'll be at the grounds shortly. The older athletes know where we usually set up camp. The new ones just follow them. Stick to the group and don't wander. I hope you all know that you aren't allowed to roam around the grounds. If you are leaving the group, it will only be for your event and you will be accompanied by one of the teachers. No one leaves unattended. Am I clear?' yelled Shagun, looking very serious.

The girls nodded their assent. Shagun walked over to Arthi and looked down at her from her great height. The fact that Arthi was seated made her seem even smaller.

'I hope I won't have any trouble from you,' she asked sternly.

Arthi was startled by Shagun's sudden intervention. She knew why she was being singled out.

'No, Shagun! I won't do anything stupid,' she said, red-faced.

Shagun nodded her approval and gave Noorie a warning look as well and then left to join her group.

The girls didn't have much time to dwell on their dark moment of the day because the bus rounded a turn and the seniors cheered as the MRC grounds came into view. Somebody started singing the school anthem and soon everyone joined in, singing with pride and zeal. Noorie and Arthi stared in frank appreciation at the immaculate grounds and its vibrant green surroundings.

The emerald oval shone in the morning sun. The grass was well trimmed and lay like a carpet of velvet from end to end. The red mud track that surrounded the oval was marked with white powder into six tracks that ran around the green. Galleries of grey concrete flanked three sides of the grounds. A large pavilion stood in the centre of the fourth side, facing the centre of the oval. It was lined with chairs and large rugs, and in the first row, there were leather sofas and coffee tables. A podium stood to one side of the pavilion, with an impressive-looking mike and sound system. Speakers were hung up on several poles around the grounds and some kind of military music blared out. A gentle breeze swished the leaves of the many eucalyptus, pine, and fir trees that stood like silent sentinels around the MRC grounds. The air smelt fresh and clean.

A few young men in khaki shorts, white T-shirts, and black shoes ran around, making final adjustments to the score board, sound system, and sports equipment. Three of them carried a freshly painted white victory stand to the centre of the oval. The numbers 1, 2, and 3 stood out boldly in black on the three steps of the victory stand. Arthi and Noorie gazed in mounting awe at their surroundings. Other schools had also arrived and the galleries were filling up fast. The air was filled with chatter, hoots, laughter, and cheers. The two girls tried to identify the various schools they had heard so much about. They picked out the Josephites, attired in blue and white, warming up at the far end of the field. They saw the all-whites from James Lawrence fooling around in the gallery. A flash of gold caught their eye as the formidable team from St George's passed their spot. There were no smiles or cheers in their group. They looked dead serious.

'They look hard-core!' whispered Arthi.

'Did you see their muscles? I mean, one of the girls' calf muscles stood out like rocks! And another one had bulging biceps like a guy's!' said Noorie, wide-eyed.

'Our champs look puny next to them! They look like bloody wrestlers!' replied Arthi.

The senior athletes had also noted the muscular golden team that took its place next to them in the galleries. If they were awed or threatened, they didn't show it, for they didn't want the juniors to panic. The school team sat on the same side as the pavilion and so they couldn't see the opening ceremony. They just heard the prayers, songs, and speeches on the many speakers. It was all over in half an hour, for the entire crowd was here for the sports and not the speeches.

'Sub-junior girls' 100-m heats in exactly five minutes! All participants please report to 100-m track immediately. Juniors' long jumps heats will happen simultaneously. Inter girls' high jumps will begin at 10.30 a.m. High jumpers, please report to the high-jump pit immediately. Seniors' shot-put heats will be underway shortly as well,' announced a voice with a fancy British accent.

'And so it begins,' said Shagun with a smile. 'Girls! I want you to give your best today. Don't worry about the results. Just go out there and do what you were meant to do, what you have been training for all these weeks.

Do us proud!' She pumped her fists in the air and the athletes gathered around and cheered.

The rest of the day was a blur for Arthi and Noorie. Though they weren't participating, they were kept busy running around giving water, glucose powder, and biscuits to the athletes who were competing for various events at different parts of the field. Gunshots rang out in the air every time a sprint began; the first one had startled Noorie out of her skin, for she had never heard one before. Arthi had laughed as Noorie jumped up in her seat, looking terrified.

There were two or three heats for most of the track events like 100 m, 200 m, 400 m, and 800 m. The Juniors only had 100 m and 200 m, and both Seema and Gayathri had competed for them. And thankfully, they had both qualified even though they had both come in at third place only. They would be there in the finals tomorrow, but it would be a tough one because there were four other girls who were already faster than them.

'I feel hopeless,' mumbled Seema. 'Even if I run my fastest, I won't be able to outrun the others. That means I'll just come fifth or, worse, last!'

Gayathri just sat with a dark look on her face. She was dejected. Coach Rhonda tried to motivate them and cheer them up.

'Girls! Don't give up like this! So the others did better today. But you will do better tomorrow. That girl from St George's who came second in your group, Gayathri, is not even as fast as you. You can do better. Your time during practice is much better than what hers was today. You were probably nervous and that's why you didn't run your fastest today. So surprise them and show them what you've got at the finals!'

'My time is better than hers? Really?' asked Gayathri, looking up, a glimmer of hope in her eyes.

'Would I lie to you, child?' asked Coach.

'No, ma'am! Of course not! You wouldn't!' replied Gayathri, smiling.

Coach patted her back and nodded at Seema as well and left to encourage the throwers. There was quite a crowd near the discus trials. There was just one participant from each school and so there were no heats for it. It was the finals straightaway. A strong muscular girl from St George's grunted as she threw the discus high and far into the distance. The volunteers ran with the tape to measure the distance of the throw. Shambhavi, a slender senior, was representing Royal Academy for Young Women, and it was her first time. She took a shaky breath and moved into the circle from within which she was expected to throw the discus. She focused on the technique Coach Rhonda had taught her, to use her weight, momentum, and strength in perfect balance to swing the discus as far off as possible. She closed her eyes for a moment and tried to shut out the din around her. Taking a deep breath, she moved her feet and body in tandem while she used the strength of her arm to whip out the discus from under her fingers. The crowd watched as the discus flew low but far and landed at a spot just after the St George's girl had hit. Shambhavi whooped and jumped in the air and hugged Coach Rhonda when she landed. The bull-like girl from St George's grunted at her in anger. It was going quite well after all. She was a slender girl but looks could be deceptive.

At another corner of the field, the Inter girls were getting ready for their high jumps. The horizontal pole was placed at a height of 1 m above the ground. The girl from James Lawrence was a tiny one, just over five feet tall, and she looked like a miniature next to the mammoth from Nilgiris High. Aparna from class 8 was competing for Royal Academy for Young Women, and she was a chubby, stocky girl. But that hadn't stopped her from winning the Junior high jump last year. She had done exceptionally well and her competitors looked at her with a mix of respect and fear. Coach knew Aparna had a good chance to win this year as well, and her intuition became reality as she watched Aparna soar over the pole with a grace that belied her chunkiness.

'She'll break the record this year,' thought the coach in admiration.

And she did just that. She won the Inter high jumps and broke last year's record with ease. She smiled shyly as her fellow athletes crowded around her, congratulating her for her stellar performance.

Noorie and Arthi watched as the volunteers set up the hurdles for the 100-m hurdles heats. All categories would have a go at it in quick succession and then the hurdles would be removed from the tracks. Shagun was at the senior level, and their heat was first. The school team was silent as they watched their games captain take position and they crossed their fingers, hoping for a good result. Shagun's competition looked equally competent. They were all tall and long-limbed like her. The girl from St Joseph's wore tiny blue shorts that made her look like she was all legs and nothing else. She had short hair like a boy, and she said something to Shagun and gave her a nasty smile, trying to haze her. Shagun just looked ahead and refused to respond.

'On your marks! Get set! *Go*!' yelled the khaki-clad volunteer as he shot the gun.

The six girls leapt from the start line and moved gracefully ahead like a pack of gazelles. The crowd watched in breathless amazement as all of them moved in tandem. They were well matched.

'Come on, Shagun!' yelled one of the girls from their team.

'Up up! Shagun!' yelled another.

The air was filled with shouts and screams as each school cheered for their athlete. The girls watched as slowly but surely the Josephite girl and Shagun took the lead. They were running neck to neck and leaping over the hurdles, mirroring each other's motions.

'Oh my God! Oh my God!' whispered one of the girls near Noorie.

They were nearing the end, just two more hurdles to cross and a few meters ahead lay the finish line. The crowd roared as both the girls flew over the remaining hurdles and crossed the finish line together.

'What a race! What a race!' yelled Ms Shobha.

Coach Rhonda was already at the finish line, hugging Shagun.

The performance of the Inters and Juniors was not good and they didn't qualify, much to Coach's regret. But Seema did very well for the Juniors and she glowed with happiness. The day was almost drawing to an end. Coach went over to the pavilion to collect the final list which would have the names of all the girls who had qualified for the finals for the next day. Their performance had been good but not exemplary. There were a few events for which they had failed to qualify, which had been a disappointment. Every point counted when it came to the finals. And the more events they had, the more they could score. Coach and Shagun discussed the finals list in the bus, and their expressions turned grim. There was no way they would get the first place, it seemed. St Joseph's was firmly in the lead. They had done exceptionally well as always. And St George's followed them with their stellar performance that day. Royal Academy for Young Women looked to be third place now, and there was no guarantee of that tomorrow because James Lawrence was doing quite well (surprisingly!).

'Girls! It's going to be a tight one tomorrow. We have to win each and every event. Congratulations to all the jumpers and throwers. You all did very well today. All those who have qualified for the finals for the track events, make sure you are well rested today. Go back, eat well, and sleep well. Don't do anything stupid and hurt yourself, OK?' yelled Shagun over the rumble of the bus.

The girls mumbled yes and sat tiredly in their seats. They were all quite exhausted after the day and couldn't wait to get back to school and their beds.

There was a small crowd in the front yard waiting to receive them. A few teachers and both the heads of the school and boarding stood atop the steps, waiting for news from the athletes. Shagun and Coach Rhonda got off the bus first to update the sisters. Sr. Rosemary looked grim as she heard the news. She had been hoping for a better performance. She had wanted the school to come in first place and bring home the trophy, and now it looked like it was a distant dream.

'At least try to come in the top three, Coach! Else it's just disgraceful! Disgraceful!' she snapped.

'Yes, Sister,' mumbled the coach, looking downcast.

The athletes trudged in tiredly with their spikes and blazers. They dragged themselves to the hot showers and made it to the dining hall for dinner. All the others had finished theirs and were already on the way to the dorms. But the sight of food perked up even the weariest child. The centre table was loaded with goodies. Huge red pieces of tandoori chicken were piled up on a large steel plate. There were large steaming bowls of a rich-looking dal makhani and vegetable jalfrezi. Piles of rotis sat on another plate. A large steel dish full of hot peas pulao beckoned the girls.

'Wow! I mean! Just wow! Wow!' said Arthi.

The girls were so hungry. They had all been too tense to eat their packed lunches of chicken sandwiches, and all that hot food reminded them how starved they were. The girls piled their plates with the delicious food and took their seats at the tables. Between mouthfuls, they discussed their performance at the MRC grounds that day.

'Whoever is in the finals has to do really, really well!' said Noorie as she dug into her tandoori chicken leg.

'It's easy for you to say that! You aren't there for anything, now are you?' replied Seema.

'Umm . . . umm . . . I didn't mean it like that, Seema. I was just saying . . .' mumbled a chastised Noorie.

'Don't . . . just don't say anything. We are already tense . . . we don't need you to remind us again and again,' mumbled Seema, looking away.

Arthi opened her mouth to say something but Noorie shook her head, quietly asking her to keep mum. They had to be supportive now. They could only imagine the pressure these girls were under.

'Seema, Gayathri, get to bed early today, all right?' said Shagun, walking over to their table. She smiled at Arthi and Noorie and left the dining hall.

Their classmates were brushing their teeth and getting ready for bed when the athletes reached the Yellow Dorm. They crowded around the girls, hungry for news about the day. As the storytelling grew more and more exaggerated the *oohs* and *aahs* in the crowd increased until Annie Nanny came out of her room to yell at the girls to shut up and go to bed. She turned off the lights and threatened to throw out anyone who so much as hiccupped. The girls giggled as they got under their covers. Noorie and the others fell asleep almost as soon as their heads touched the pillows for they were bone-weary tired after all the excitement and action at the MRC grounds. That night the dreams in Yellow Dorm were vivid and victorious as they won trophy after trophy, medal after medal and brought glory to their alma mater.

# Chapter 12

# THE FINALS

The grey clouds lent an ominous air to the MRC grounds on the day of the finals. The pale sun struggled to show his face. A light drizzle made everyone bring out their umbrellas and raincoats. The temperature had dropped too as a cold wind whipped the girls and boys in the open field. The athletes sat huddled in the rain, shivering. It was an awful day to be out in the open running. But there was no other way around it. Seema was highly strung and so was Gayathri. The pressure was getting to the younger ones. They didn't talk to anyone and just sat quietly next to one another in silent support.

Hurdles would be the first event, and the track had already been prepared by the time they arrived. Shagun stood with the other finalists on the start line, jumping up and down, trying to keep warm. She had a knot of tension in her belly that refused to go away.

'I have to win this! I have to!' she whispered fiercely to herself.

She wanted to have a win first thing in the morning, not just to get the points but to elevate the mood of her team. She could see they were down in the dumps. A win would get their spirits high and would bring back the confidence that was much needed today.

'Half the battle will be won then,' she thought.

The drizzle was persistent and irritating. It made her cold and wet and uncomfortable. The mud track was getting a bit mushy too. She could see puddles forming here and there, and she hoped there weren't any in her track. It would affect her balance and momentum if there were any changes in the ground level. She prayed for a good race, no, a *great* race!

'On your marks! Get set! *Go*!' yelled the volunteer. The gunshot rang out in the field, and the first event of the day was underway with a roar from the galleries. Shagun's team watched breathlessly as she jumped and ran with the determination of a cheetah. The Josephite from yesterday had the lead, and they watched Shagun overtake the others and close the gap midway through the race.

'Sha-gun! Sha-gun! Shag-un!' chanted the girls in one ear-shattering voice. They were beside themselves with excitement and terror. The two girls were running neck and neck just like the previous day. They could hear the Josephites cheering from the other end for their girl. And then suddenly the Josephite slipped a little and lost a precious second or two, trying to regain her balance. But that was all Shagun wanted; she pounded ahead and zoomed to the finish line, winning the first gold of the day. Maybe the rain wasn't such a bad thing after all!

Shagun's team leapt up from the stands. Shouting, laughing, cheering and dancing! They were so happy, so happy that some of them began to cry. Shagun looked up from the finish line and she saw a few of her team members throwing up their umbrellas and jumping up and down, doing some weird tribal or Red Indian dance and she laughed with relief.

'Thank you, God! Thank you!' she whispered.

Her team's confidence had been patched up and there was a fire in their belly again. All was not hopeless, and she knew it was the *just* the beginning they were looking for that day. She felt bad for her opponent who had slipped but they did need the points more than St Joseph's after all, and perhaps this was what they called *divine intervention*.

'Junior girls 100 m! To the start line, please!' yelled the announcer with her clipped accent.

Seema and Gayathri were already on their way to the start line together. The others watched tensely as they took their places. The shot pierced the air, and the girls hit the tracks with a vengeance.

'Come on! Seema! Gayathri! Come on, girls!'

'You can do it!'

'Up, up, girls!'

The screams rang out as the two girls in brown raced ahead with the others. Midway through the race, two athletes broke from the pack and took the lead, the girl from St Joseph's and one from St George's.

'Oh, no!' groaned Coach.

Seema and Gayathri were still in the middle of the pack. And then Gayathri inched ahead as the group approached the finish line. The crowd screamed as the Josephite and St George's athletes cleared as first and second. There was a girl from James Lawrence a second or two behind Gayathri.

'Oh my God!' whispered Arthi, too tense to breathe as she watched.

Gayathri was almost at the finish line when the James Lawrence girl took a giant leap and landed at the finish line a nanosecond before Gayathri. The Royal Academy for Young Women team had been on their feet cheering her on, but when they saw the near-victory snatched away from them, they sat down in shock.

'That was so close, so close!' whispered Noorie, shaking her head.

Coach Rhonda was holding a sobbing Gayathri while Seema, who had come in fifth, stood aside stiffly. They tried to console Gayathri, who was beside herself with grief. The team didn't say anything when the girls got back to their seats. No one wanted to create a fuss. Winning and losing was part and parcel of sports after all.

They were watching the Inter girls 100 m sprint. Their runner came in second place for both 100 m and 200 m, and their points on the scoreboard slowly inched upward, much to their relief. The Senior 200 m also went well, with Sonali securing first place. Noorie looked at the scoreboard and squinted at the points through the sheet of rain.

St Josephs—232, St Georges—228, Royal Academy for Young Women—198, James Lawrence—196

The girls in brown groaned as the James Lawrence runner overtook theirs for the Senior 400-m event.

'Oh, crap! Now they are in third place!' screamed Shagun.

Shoulders began to slump, hands slapped foreheads in frustration, and feet kicked angrily at nearby rocks and stones. The team's morale was down again. James Lawrence had now displaced them to fourth place with their recent win. That was the last individual event and all that remained was the 4×100-m relay for all categories.

'Girls! Girls! Chin up! Let's not give up, please! We still have the relay to make up in points. Let's try to come first for each and every one, and we will be able save the situation!' pleaded Shambhavi.

Shagun, Coach Rhonda, and Ms Shobha gathered the relay runners into a huddle and discussed strategy. They broke up after a few minutes, and Shagun called Arthi.

'I want you, Seema, as the first runner for the relay team, and I want you, Arthi, to be last runner. Can you do it?' she asked, looking into Arthi's eyes.

'Me?' she squeaked.

'Yes, you! You are a fresh face. They don't know you. You are as good as Seema, and Gayathri is in no state to run. She has already given up after her loss. I can't take any chances now. I believe you can run better. Will you do it, Arthi?' she asked.

Arthi looked up at Shagun's serious brown eyes and furrowed brow. Her games captain looked so sure of herself and yet so tense. Arthi knew this was her chance to shine but she wasn't confident enough.

'You think I can do it, Shagun?' she asked, doubt lacing her words.

'Absolutely! I've seen you run. And you have that fire in your belly which I need at this moment. I know you won't let me down. You won't let your school down!' she said, squeezing Arthi's hand.

'OK! I'll . . . I'll do it! I'll run!'

'Excellent!' shouted Shagun, and she gave Arthi a hug and little kiss on her forehead.

Arthi turned red with pleasure. She had always admired Shagun and now her idol was giving her a chance to prove her worth and she wouldn't let her down. Seema, however, didn't look too pleased but she held her tongue.

Arthi took her place beside the other athletes from various schools when it was her turn to run for the relay. The 400-m oval track was divided into four portions— two curves and two straight portions. The first and third runners would run on the curves while the second and fourth runners would be doing their sprinting on the straight portions of the track. They drew lots for the tracks and Arthi's team was allotted the sixth track, which was the outermost and would challenge Seema the most. But she would also be placed ahead of the other runners so she could take the lead and get their team ahead in the beginning itself. The other teams were surprised to see Seema as the first runner and a nobody as the last runner. Some of the athletes smirked mockingly at Arthi.

'Who are you?' a girl in golden uniform asked Arthi. 'Where is Gayathri?'

Arthi didn't say anything. She was so nervous that her stomach was tied up in knots. She prayed and prayed she wouldn't do anything silly like drop the baton and get disqualified. The gunshot jolted her out of her tension and she watched, with rising hope, Seema fly like bird on the red muddy track. Flecks of mud flew in all directions as she ran with a vengeance. She had a great lead, and she passed on the baton to the second runner, who ran as fast as she could in the drizzle that threatened to blind her because of the wind direction. She veered close to the edge of the track and the home team gasped, hoping she wouldn't be disqualified. The Josephite girl was at her heels. She had caught up with her by the time she finished her leg of the track. The third runner grabbed the baton and ran towards Arthi. The lead that Seema had managed to grasp was slipping out of their fingers. The Josephite girl in blue overtook her, and the golden athlete caught up with her. When the baton was thrust into Arthi's outstretched hand, there were two girls already in front of her. She started sprinting. The wind poured the light rain right into her eyes, stinging them. She could see the two girls ahead, and she heard a pounding behind her as someone caught up. She glanced from the corner of her eye and saw she was running in tandem with the James Lawrence girl.

'No! I can't let them win!' she thought.

The finish line loomed ahead. The other two girls were almost there. Arthi and the James Lawrence girl ran shoulder to shoulder, matching their steps as the crowd roared in excitement. Arthi could only hear her heart pumping in her ears. And just as she neared the finish line, she stuck her upper body forward and crossed it a split second before James Lawrence.

The team from the Royal Academy for Young Women threw up their hands in delight and started dancing in the rain.

'We won! We won!' they shouted.

And indeed they had. The Juniors relay win had secured them a third place in the overall points tally, and they had Arthi to thank for her fast feet and quick thinking.

Noorie clapped so hard her hands were almost red and sore. Her throat was hoarse with all the shouting and singing but she was so happy. Her friend stood on the victory stand, a bronze medal hanging on her proud chest. She felt almost as if it was her win too.

And with a bang, the inter-school sports were over, and it was time for the final march-past. The girls stood three in a line, one behind the other with Shagun leading them, school flag in her hand. The rain had stopped thankfully and the sun was about to set. The school team was ready for the victory march. The victors took their places, and the Royal Academy for Young Women was the third school among the girls to march the victory lap on the MRC tracks.

Noorie's heart was so full of pride for her school and her team that she felt it would burst. She stamped her feet and swung her arms in perfect coordination with the drumbeats. The girls in brown had done well. Shagun held the flag high, and the brown and cream colours danced gaily in the evening breeze. The band struck up the school song as they neared the pavilion. They all turned to their right and raised their hands to their foreheads to salute the chief guest, a senior army officer who stood in all his military finery. Noorie also saw both Sr. Rosemary and Sr. Josephine behind the chief guest, their faces wreathed in smiles. The girls marched on, heads held high in pride.

Someone distributed bars of Dairy Milk chocolate in the bus, and the girls happily wolfed them down. The bus roared through the hairpin bends, taking them past Ketti Valley. It was almost dark, and the hills were studded with lights. Noorie got a glimpse of the grotto, and she smiled, thinking of what she had prayed for. She had asked for a medal for Arthi. It looked like the grotto had some magic after all.

# Chapter 13

# THE FARM

'Girls, today, as a part of our geography lesson, we will be visiting the school farm,' announced Ms Rani.

All the girls sat up in the seats and looked very interested. The school farm lay behind the back compound and extended for several acres. It was off limits for the students, and the high picket fence with its permanently locked gate kept them out. Jenna had told them about the farm, and both Noorie and Arthi were excited to see it. They were both city girls and had never been on a working farm before. The only animals they had seen other than the occasional dog, cat, and cow were in pictures and the TV. Jenna was a member of the gardening club last year, and she had visited the farm with Sr. Elizabeth, who ran the club. She was a jolly nun who was a nature lover and could be seen pottering about in the school and convent gardens at all hours. Though she came across as clumsy and absent-minded, she had a doctorate in agriculture and was much revered by the environmentalists in Ooty. The farm was directly under her control, and she made all the important decisions regarding its crops and animals.

'Now, Sr. Elizabeth will be giving us a tour. She is very kind to take time from her busy schedule to do this. I want all of you to behave well. We will walk in twos, and everyone must stick to the group. No wandering about and getting lost. Am I clear?' asked Ms Rani, looking around with a stern eye.

Priya was signing to Arthi, making some private plans during the farm tour and Ms Rani caught her red-handed.

'And what are you signing about?' she asked, pulling Priya up in her seat.

'You are up to no good and I'm sure you're trying to rope in Arthi for some no-good mischief, aren't you?' Ms Rani continued.

Priya stood up, claiming her innocence, and looked at Ms Rani, making puppy-dog eyes.

'Oh no, you don't!' laughed Ms Rani, who knew exactly what Priya was trying to achieve. 'You can't fool me. You will stay by my side during the tour.'

Priya sat down defeated. It was going to be boring tour then, if she was going to be stuck by the teacher's side. She had been hoping to explore the farm with Arthi or anyone else who was game enough to have some adventure.

The girls quickly stood in pairs and made their way to the back compound, bubbling with excitement. Noorie and Arthi walked side by side, holding hands. Sr. Elizabeth was waiting for them near the fence.

The girls looked at her in amazement. Gone were her typical white and black nun's habit, and instead she was wearing dark-blue workman's overalls and a large straw hat that almost covered her face. Her black gumboots were smeared with mud and some other green goo. She looked more like a farmhand than a nun! She smiled warmly as the girls approached. She loved children but she loved plants and animals a whole lot more.

'Good morning, girls! It's a bright and sunny morning after a week of rain. We will be touring the school farm today. How many of you have already seen it before?' enquired Sr. Elizabeth.

Jenna's hand shot up in the air. She was the only one, it seemed.

'Hello, Jenna, come on up. You can walk with me then,' she invited a gleeful Jenna, who loved being in the limelight.

'Now, girls, we can't see all of the farm in one hour, so I will just show some of the interesting areas, keeping in mind the need for your education and also for your appreciation and respect for nature. As you know, we grow almost all the fruits and vegetables for our consumption here in our fields themselves. Very rarely do we buy any from the Ooty Municipal Market. We use the best seeds and cultivation techniques to ensure you have the best produce on your plates. All these are grown with minimal use of pesticides, fungicides, and chemical fertilizers. I believe in *organic* farming. Have any of you heard of this?' She paused, waiting for an answer, but receiving none, she continued, 'It's a concept that's very much in vogue in Europe, where I recently attended the International Agriculture Convention. And I am using these new techniques right here in our school farm. Not many other farms in India use these techniques yet, but you girls have the benefit of my wisdom, eh?' she chuckled happily.

The girls had never heard of organic farming before, but since it was European, they were very impressed.

'So the next time we eat our vegetables and fruits, we must do so with greater *respect*,' said Arthi, snorting with laughter.

'Shh! She'll hear you!' whispered Noorie.

'Don't be such a bore! Live a little!' muttered Arthi, giving her a nudge.

Sr. Elizabeth led them to a large shed with a thatched roof. The girls walked carefully as the paths were slippery and muddy after the rains. They took care not to soil their shoes and socks too much by avoiding the large muddy puddles. The cowshed was enormous, and the girls smelt it before they saw it. They scrunched up their noses at the strong smell of cow dung. Only Sr. Elizabeth seemed untouched by it while the others hurriedly pulled out their hankies and buried their noses in these.

'We have over fifty cows here. Most of them are Jersey cows and they give about ten litres of milk every day. Those young men there are the cowhands who milk the cows every morning, and they also clean the shed and feed the cows. Come on, let's go inside!' said Sr. Elizabeth.

Sreedevi and Savita refused to come in, saying it was too dirty and smelly. Ms Rani hissed at them and pulled them inside and asked them to stop making a fuss.

'But, Miss! She is a princess! She doesn't visit cowsheds!' said Savita, horrified.

'I don't care if she is a queen. In my class she is just like rest. So stop fussing and come inside immediately!' snapped Ms Rani, her face turning purple.

Savita and Sreedevi followed reluctantly, all the while making gagging sounds and pretending to vomit. Meanwhile, Noorie watched the cows in fascination. There were rows and rows of them of many colours and sizes: black, white, brown, patchy, large, small, and medium. Their eyes were large, wet, and expressive. Their horns were trimmed and their coats shone. The cowshed had a high ceiling and was relatively clean. Large cauldrons of cattle feed and piles of freshly cut grass lay in orderly lines before the cows.

'Look! Look! Real-life cowboys!' said Arthi with a laugh.

Noorie looked up excitedly but she realized Arthi was just poking fun at the cowhands. They were simple local men dressed in worn-out blue sweaters, patched-up pants, and dirty gumboots. They looked nothing like the dashing cowboys they read about in Louis L'Amour books.

Sr. Elizabeth droned on about the milk production capabilities of the cows and the butterfat content and the feed they were given and so on. Her words flitted around Noorie, who was not paying any attention. She just watched the cows silently chewing and chewing away to glory.

The next stop was the dairy hall, a large spotless hall with complicated-looking steel appliances, huge stoves, and long steel tables and vessels. A few nuns in crisp white habits bustled about in the dairy hall, doing their daily chores. They hardly paused to greet the girls. Sr. Elizabeth explained to the girls how butter and cheese were made right here for their use. As the girls walked around in awe they saw huge slabs of freshly made pale golden-yellow butter and large rings of cheese being prepared.

'Our sisters from Amsterdam and Switzerland were the ones who started dairy farming in our convent. This dairy hall is more than fifty years old. Sr. Anna and Sr. Petra were the pioneers of dairy farming here,' said Sr. Elizabeth pointing at the pictures of two severe-looking nuns on the wall. 'Over the years, we have improved our techniques and increased our yield of both butter and cheese. Most of it is consumed by the boarders and the sisters in the convent and whatever remains is given to the bishop's house in Ooty.' Jenna, the butter lover, could hardly drag herself away from the mountains of butter and had to be forcibly removed from the dairy hall by an embarrassed Ms Rani.

The crowd walked ahead, wondering where Sr. Elizabeth would take them next.

'She's taking us to the pigsty!' yelled Jenna from somewhere up front.

Noorie had never seen a pig before and she was excited. She hoped there were piglets too.

'Will they be pink and squeaky like in the cartoons?' she wondered.

The girls walked over to a large walled enclosure. The stone wall was as high as their chests, and they peered over to see the inhabitants. Noorie gasped as she saw a huge sow standing near a trough at far end of the yard. She was enormous and she had over ten little piglets sucking from her many teats.

'Oh my God! That's disgusting!' yelled Arthi, voicing Noorie's exact thoughts.

The black-and-white sow made low grunting noises and put her head inside the trough, obviously eating something in it, while her piglets tugged at her teats impatiently.

'The piglets are kinda cute though,' murmured Noorie, who was getting over the initial shock of seeing the gigantic sow standing on the mushy black earth. The piglets were tiny and were pink, black, and a patchy black-and-white. They fought with each other for their mother's milk while she continued eating with gusto from the trough.

'What is she eating, Sister?' asked Myra.

'Oh, she eats almost everything!' said Sr. Elizabeth enthusiastically. 'Grass, leaves, vegetables, leftovers, grains, old bread, and so on.'

'Can you give it meat?' asked one of the girls.

'No! We don't feed the pig meat at all,' replied Sr. Elizabeth.

'What about shit, Sister? Do they eat shit?' asked someone.

The girls gasped and looked around to see who asked the question. It was Priya and she was grinning from ear to ear at Sr. Elizabeth's outraged expression.

'No, young lady! We *do not* feed our pigs any *excreta*!' she yelled, going red in the ears. She looked at Ms Rani accusingly as though she had taught Priya all this nonsense. A red-faced Ms Rani asked Priya to leave the group and return to class immediately. Priya just shrugged and left nonchalantly. She was grinning happily because shocking others was something she truly enjoyed.

'Young girls these days, I tell you! No respect at all! And no intelligence in their heads! Morons!' mumbled Sr. Elizabeth angrily while Ms Rani ran ahead to mollify her.

The girls giggled at the drama and continued to watch the antics of the piglets. A few of them had left their mother now and were squealing and jumping about in the wet mud. They ran around squeaking and rolling in the dirty puddles thoroughly enjoying themselves. The girls laughed and laughed as the piglets emerged black and brown from the muddy puddles. And throughout all this the fat sow just kept her head down, eating without a care in the world.

'I guess we now know the real meaning of *pigging out*,' said Noorie.

'Yeah! And *hogging*,' replied Arthi giggling.

A farmhand with three dogs on leashes approached them. He tipped his hat to Sr. Elizabeth, said something in Tamil, and walked away.

'What beautiful dogs!' exclaimed Myra. She loved dogs but her parents weren't fond of them and so she never had a chance to keep one as a pet. The German shepherds, with healthy, shiny coats, ran on ahead, keeping the farmhand on his toes. She went over to Sr. Elizabeth to find out more of the farm dogs.

The group then moved on to a green pasture with gentle undulating hills and valleys. A large flock of sheep frolicked in the lush green grass under the watchful eye of a shepherd dressed in a faded old sweater that had seen better days. He ran over to them when he saw Sr. Elizabeth. His face was dirty but his smile was warm and sincere. They spoke for a few minutes and then Sr. Elizabeth turned to the girls.

'We have something interesting to show you girls,' she said with a smile and took them to the barn that stood a few yards away.

Once their eyes got used to the darkness of the barn, the girls gasped in delight at the sight before them. Five of the ewes had given birth and there were seven little lambs in the hay. Some of them were suckling, a few were trying to stand up and take unsteady steps, and one lay curled up in the hay, eyes closed.

'Oh! So cute!'

'How adorable!'

'I want to take one home!'

'I have never seen anything so delightful!'

The joyful cries of the girls rang out in the barn as they crowded around the ewes and lambs though at a safe distance.

'Quiet! Quiet! You'll frighten them!' Sr. Elizabeth hushed them. The rest of their elation was muted but the girls just couldn't get enough of the cuteness of the lambs.

Sr. Elizabeth said that newborn lambs were very delicate and almost 20 per cent of them didn't make it. She explained that the greatest killer was starvation.

'In case something happens to the mother, we take to bottle-feeding the lamb. But thankfully none of the ewes were hurt in birth!' she continued.

The girls watched Mother Nature at her gentlest moment. They saw the ewes licking their young lambs and keeping them close and warm.

'Sister, can we come and watch a birth next time?' asked a curious Myra.

'Ha ha! Sure! Sure! If you are interested, why not? It's always good to know how nature works. What's your name, child?' she asked.

'Myra, Sister,' she replied.

'I'll keep you in mind,' she said.

'Can we see the horses, Sister?' asked Jenna.

'Of course we will, dear. I'll take you to the stables next,' replied Sr. Elizabeth.

The stables were a large establishment in itself. There were many men working in it. Most of the horses were inside, though a few were running around in the corral. Black, brown, and chestnut-coloured horses with shiny coats and streaming manes stood in their stalls. The stallions were several hands high, and the girls were awed by their size and speed as they ran around in the corral. A few quiet mares were being led into the stables after their morning chores in the farm. They were shorter and chunkier, unlike the sleek stallions. The girls laughed when they saw two ponies running in the nearby meadow.

'It looks like they're playing catch!' exclaimed Radhica.

'Oh! Ponies are very playful and they get into all sorts of trouble, mind you. We always have to keep a stern eye on them,' replied Sr. Elizabeth, watching the ponies fondly. 'Perhaps you girls can sign up for horse riding next term.'

'Oh! I would really love that!' exclaimed Jenna.

The girls walked over to the fields. The gentle slopes of the hills at the back of the school had been converted into terraces on which several crops were planted.

'They look like giant steps, don't they?' said Arthi.

'Here we grow a wide variety of vegetables like carrots, cabbages, lettuce, potatoes, radishes, turnips, and so on. The British introduced most of these crops in Ooty. These are not indigenous to Ooty, you see. I don't know if you girls are aware, but Ooty was the summer capital of the Madras presidency under British rule and several establishments started by the British are still maintained and used by the local population and tourists,' explained Sr. Elizabeth in her tour-guide voice.

The girls admired the neat rows of green plants that grew on the terraces in perfect order.

'What about fruits, Sister? Do we grow any?' asked Myra.

'Of course we do. We have orchards a little ahead, near the convent side. We grow apples, plums, litchis, pears, and peaches. You'll find most of them on your plate throughout the year,' she said, winking at her.

'Oh! But I'm a day scholar, Sister,' replied Myra shyly.

'Ah! Perhaps you should become a boarder just to eat our fruits and vegetables. They are far more delicious than the ones you buy at the Ooty market, dear,' she said with a smile.

Myra laughed at that and shook her head.

'It's time to go back, girls!' said Ms Rani, suddenly glancing at her watch.

'Oh no!'

'Please! Can we stay for some more time, Ms Rani?

'Just a few more minutes, please!'

'We haven't seen the orchards yet, Miss!'

'And we haven't seen the chicken coop or the ducks or the pond!'

The girls begged and pleaded with a firm Ms Rani. But it was indeed time for the next lesson and they couldn't be late. They thanked Sr. Elizabeth profusely and were sorry to get back into their cool classrooms. They had been enjoying themselves so much in nature's lap, enjoying her bounty.

# Chapter 14

# THE PROJECT

When the students of class 7 reached their classroom that Monday morning, they saw five topics written on the blackboard in Ms Rani's perfect cursive handwriting.

PROJECT 1 FOR CLASS 7

- The freedom fighter I admire the most
- My role model (living individual)
- What makes India a secular nation?
- The Cold War
- My ancestral home

All students are asked to pick a topic and present it next week. You need to prepare at least one chart with relevant pictures/articles etc. You may also use other props. Each student will be

expected to give a 1-minute speech to
the judges explaining their topic.

There was a mixture of groans and excited chatter in
the classroom. Myra stared at the blackboard and then
copied down the topics in her rough book. She had all
week to prepare. She would think about it and make a
decision at home.

Noorie, however, had already made up her mind.
She was going to write about the Cold War. The papers
had been full of it in the beginning of the year. And her
father had insisted on explaining about the animosity
between USA and Russia. So whether she liked it or not,
her head was already half full of facts about the political
wrangling between the two superpowers. She could
speak to the librarian and access old newspapers and
related books and prepare her material. She was already
making notes about what she planned to do. She wanted
to get good marks on this project and impress Ms Rani.

Arthi, meanwhile, was irritated. She didn't have
patience for their artsy things. And all the topics
sounded a bit boring to her. Maybe she would write
about her role model. *Shagun? No! That would sound too
silly.* Perhaps she could pick some famous athlete like
P. T. Usha or Steffi Graff or Monica Seles. *Maybe she
could use this as an excuse to talk to Shagun*, she thought
smiling secretly.

'Girls, I won't be judging the project this year.
We will have a panel of judges—Sr. Rosemary, our
principal, Sr. Molly who teaches history for class 9
students, and Ms Jalu, who teaches geography for all
the senior classes.' She paused before continuing: 'I want
your work to be exemplary. This is the first time we have

a chance to show our talent to these senior teachers, so make sure you do your research well and plan it properly so that there aren't any issues in the end. Come to me if you need inspiration or help or anything at all. Don't embarrass me with shoddy work. Am I clear?'

The girls nodded and mumbled yes. Ms Rani sure seemed worked up. They got busy with the rest of classes, and no one discussed the project that day.

The school bus dropped Myra off at the top of the little hill where her home stood. There was a collection of small houses and cottages on Kurinji Malai. She stood at the bus stop for a moment taking in the quiet neighbourhood. Fresh green grass covered the slopes, a few cows mooed in the distance, yellow and white wildflowers popped out from behind rocks, smoke rose from a few chimneys, and Myra wondered what everyone was having for dinner that night.

'You know, Myra, this whole place was once covered with kurinji flowers,' her grandfather had said to her one day. 'There was a time when the hills around here were blanketed in purple-blue blossoms when flowers bloomed, once every twelve years. And the local tribes named these hills Neela-giri, which means *blue mountains*, after these very flowers! But they remind me of home . . . of the saffron flowers back home in Kashmir.'

There were no kurinji blossoms this side of the hill now though. Most of them could be seen in Mukurti National Park and other protected areas. Myra had never seen them bloom in her lifetime but she hoped she wouldn't miss the next opportunity. Her grandfather was a nature buff; he loved all sorts of plants, and their garden at home blossomed under his care. He also made it a point to take Myra for the flower show at the Ooty Botanical gardens every year in May.

Myra made her way into her room after drinking tea with her mother and grandfather. She sat down for her homework and opened her rough book. Ms Rani's words popped out from the pages. What was she going to do the project about?

'Role model? Nah! It would look too common. Freedom fighter? Hmmm . . . could be. Cold War . . . eeks . . . too boring! The secular thing sounds just as bad, something that nerd Meenu would do,' thought Myra. 'Ancestral home? But I don't really know anything of it, do I?'

She pondered over the last choice for some more time. She had never asked her father or grandfather about their ancestry or ancestral home in detail and so she just knew a few bare facts; that was all. That wouldn't be enough for a project. She would have to catch her grandfather in a chatty mood, perhaps over the weekend, and then pump him for information, she decided quietly as she turned the pages of her history textbook.

Sunday mornings after breakfast were a quiet time in the Sheikh household. Her mother was bustling about in the kitchen, busy preparing her delicious mutton biriyani, their Sunday lunch special. Her father had gone to the hospital for his medical rounds and would return only around one o'clock. Her grandfather sat outside in the front porch, rocking in his favourite armchair as he read a story to her little sister Sara. His silvery white hair glistened above the maroon woollen muffler around his neck. He wore a crisp white kurta-pyjamas and a warm olive-green sweater. His patrician features were screwed up in concentration as he read.

'Dadu', she began, 'I need your help for a school project.'

Her dadu looked up and his grey-green eyes twinkled. And when he heard her choice, he was almost as excited as a child himself. It had been a long time since he had spoken of home or his family. He rarely got a chance, as his son didn't encourage reminiscing about the past.

Dadu and Myra went up to the attic, where he pulled out some old cardboard cartons from one of the rickety old cupboards there. The dust flew up in the air, making Dadu cough. He quickly covered his nose and mouth with his large white handkerchief and asked Myra to bring the boxes down to the bedroom below. Dadu was asthmatic, and he didn't want to fall ill just when Myra wanted his help. Myra struggled down the stairs with the cartons but she was brimming with anticipation. She wondered what old stories she would discover and what treasures would be unearthed.

Once Dadu's wheezing had subsided, he asked her to open the boxes and Myra pulled out several old, crumbling photo albums. The black chart-paper-like pages were almost falling apart but the photos seemed to be in decent condition. A few silverfish scrambled out in protest as Myra turned the pages of the ancient album.

'That used to be my home,' said Dadu, pointing at an impressive wooden house set amid snow-capped peaks and surrounded by lush green trees.

'And these are my brothers and sisters.' His bony fingers gently touched a black-and-white photo. 'I haven't spoken to them in years. I don't even know if they are still . . .' he paused, 'alive.'

As Myra turned the pages, she found herself in another world, her grandfather's old world, of apple orchards and cherry trees and mulberry bushes and almond trees. He showed her the farm his father had raised them in. It had been in their family for several generations, and they all shared a love for the land. Myra laughed at the photo of five children standing near a stream. They had ear-to-ear grins and looked like they were up to all kinds of mischief.

'My brothers, sisters, and I would go to this little stream near our house and play in the evenings during summer. I still remember the taste of that water . . . so clear, so clean, so fresh. You could taste the snow of the mountain in that water, *jan*,' he said with a faraway look in his eyes.

Her great-grandparents stared at her from a large black-and-white photo. They were formally attired: him in a large black coat over his kurta-pyjamas and she wore an elaborate embroidered salwar-kameez. Her hair was covered with a light-coloured flowery scarf, and even though her lips didn't smile, you could see the smile in her eyes.

'My father was very strict. A bit of a tyrant, you could say. But my ammi, ah! She was so loving! Always kind and compassionate and constantly worrying about us.' He sighed and closed his eyes.

'Do you miss them?' asked Myra, looking up at him.

'My mother—I miss her the most! But she passed away. One of my brothers wrote to me five years ago.

But I couldn't go to the funeral. Visa issues and other political problems.'

They were quiet for some time, each busy with their own thoughts. Myra's little project had brought back a lot of memories and her dadu was wrapped up in them now.

'Why didn't you stay behind? Why did you come here?' she asked.

Dadu sighed deeply. He lay back and closed his eyes before he began.

'I used to travel frequently to cities in Pakistan and India for my father's fruit trade. On one such trip, I visited Srinagar and happened to meet a firebrand leader called Sheikh Abdullah. I attended several of his speeches and I really believed in what he was saying, about democracy and the rights of common man. I decided to join his party and I moved to Srinagar for my higher studies. My father didn't really approve of all this but I was quite adamant,' he said softly. 'One thing led to another and then I married your grandmother from Srinagar and settled down there. Later we moved to the South for better business opportunities and so here we are!'

'Did you ever see Nehru?' she asked in awe.

'No, no! Only the Sher-e-Kashmir! And my, what a lion of a man he was! But he ran into a lot of trouble with Nehru in his fight for an independent Kashmir. He was even jailed for several years, the poor man! But he was well respected in Pakistan too. Poems were written about him in Urdu. Nehru had actually sent him to Pakistan to speak to the leaders there and find a solution for Kashmir, but Nehru died in the midst of all that and so it was all scrapped.'

'So Sheikh Abdullah wanted an independent Kashmir?' asked Myra.

'Initially Sheikh Abdullah spoke for an independent Kashmir but later on, in the 1970s, he changed his tune. He then believed it would be better to *stay* with India rather than be on its own. *I* believed in this view but my family didn't. And they were quite angry with him. They were among the ones who called him a traitor. They thought he didn't keep his word because he had promised the people they could have a vote, a say in whether they wanted to be independent or not. And then he gave it all up and signed a deal with Indira Gandhi. A part of Kashmir broke off and became Azad Kashmir and it's under Pakistan's control now. Our old home and our relatives are all still there. And the Indian Kashmir is also riddled with problems and it doesn't look like a solution will be found any time soon. So there you go, a little history lesson also.'

'So . . . so we are . . . what are we then?' Myra asked hesitantly.

'Indian! We are Indian! And proud to be so!' said her dadu loudly, and his chest puffed up.

Myra smiled her relief at hearing that.

It was the morning of the presentation. The girls of class 7 were dizzy with excitement. Their charts were being put up in the assembly hall noticeboards and would be open to the whole school. Each student was allotted a certain space to place their charts and other items, if any, and they would be standing beside their exhibit to answer any questions. The main assessment would be in the afternoon, when they would be giving a short speech to the panel, classmates, and whoever else was free to attend.

Myra put up her chart with Noorie's help. Noorie gasped as she stepped back to look at her friend's handiwork. Purple saffron flowers adorned the borders of the chart, snow-capped mountains, green valleys, tumbling streams, and clear blue skies filled the body of the chart. Myra had pasted her old photographs onto this colourful background. Pictures of a bygone era showed a large three-storied house surrounded by apple trees laden with fruit, with tall snow-covered peaks looming behind it.

'The houses in the village were typically made out of unburnt bricks placed in a wooden frame made of cedar, pine, or fir. The sloping roof was covered with wooden shingles. The house was rectangular in plan and facing the south as was common there. The lower floor was for animals while the upper two floors for the residents of the house,' she explained to Noorie.

The photo of a severe-looking man in a black coat stared back at Noorie. He stood with two skinny boys and three pretty, smiling little girls beside him: Myra's great-grandfather and his children.

Myra pointed to another picture and said it had been his grandfather's city home, a large two-storied wooden house with beautiful wooden lattice windows. Another rare colour photograph captured the roof of the same house in summertime, resplendent with white and violet lilies and red tulips.

'The city houses are topped with birch bark and some earth. So in summertime, flowers usually bloomed on the roof, making it look like a garden in the sky,' explained Myra, smiling at the crowd that had gathered near her exhibit. 'My grandfather used to say that when they climbed the hills and looked down at the houses, the roofs were like bursts of colour on a green-and-brown carpet.'

A crowd of admirers had gathered around Myra's beautiful charts. It was quite unlike any of the other projects.

'And what are those trees?' asked someone pointing to another picture.

'That's cherry, those are apple near the house, and these here are walnut trees,' replied Myra. 'My grandfather's family had many orchards for growing fruits and nuts, and they used to export quite a lot during their heyday.'

The girls gazed in awe at the beautiful orchards that adorned Myra's chart. There were apricots, almonds, pears, and even grapevines. They peppered Myra with questions about her great-grandfather, his home, the life there, and his fruit business. Myra was quite flattered with all the attention and answered their questions with gusto.

'And now? Where are they all now? Here?' asked Arthi.

'My grandfather is the only one who moved to India. The rest of his brothers and sisters are all still there. But we aren't in touch with them,' she replied.

'And *where* did you say this was?' asked someone sharply.

'It's a little village near Muzzafarabad,' replied Myra, looking for the owner of the voice.

Sreedevi stepped forward, her eyes blazing. She had drawn herself up to her full height that was considerable for a twelve-year-old, as she was almost a head taller than all the other girls. She looked down her regal nose and curled her lip in disgust.

'So then you're a Pakistani!' she said spitefully.

Myra went white with shock. The other girls in the crowd gasped and took a step back at the attack. They all looked at Myra in mounting alarm.

'No! I'm not! I'm . . . I'm Indian! I was born in Ooty, not Pakistan,' said Myra, her voice shaking.

Sreedevi shook her head vehemently and pointed a slim finger at Myra and said, 'No! You aren't! Your people are still there. You said so yourself. *You* are a Pakistani!'

Myra's lower lip trembled.

'No! No! I'm not! I'm not!' Her voice dropped to a whisper and two large teardrops rolled down her rosy cheeks.

'Go back to your own country! Go back! You have no place here!' yelled Sreedevi.

Myra broke down; she opened her mouth to say something, but no words could be heard. The girls slowly moved away from Myra, as if she had something contagious. Even Noorie and Arthi had stepped back involuntarily during the attack.

'*This* place she talks about is *not* in India any more. It's in *Pakistan-occupied Kashmir*. They call it *Azad Kashmir*. They wanted to be free of us, of us Indians! So they left us and joined Pakistan. Do you know that?' announced a furious Sreedevi.

'I am from Kashmir. My family is related to the old maharaja there. My family has told me all about the people who didn't want to belong to India, who wanted to be free from India. You are not Kashmiri or even

Indian. Your people left India and went, so how dare you come here and think you are one of us?'

Sreedevi turned her heel and left, leaving her angry words hanging in the air. She was still seething with anger. It was obvious that this was an issue close to her heart. Meanwhile Myra was left sobbing near her charts.

'It's OK. Just ignore her. It will be OK,' consoled Noorie, who had stayed behind while all the others left with Sreedevi. 'She is just saying some old stuff. It doesn't matter.'

Myra shook her head sadly. Her worst fears were coming true. Sreedevi had exposed her deepest doubts in one stroke. There was some truth in what she had said after all. Her extended family still continued to live in their family home in Muzaffarabad even though her grandfather had moved to India. And Sreedevi's accusation that she was *not an Indian* tore at her very core.

Myra passed the rest of the day in a daze. She barely managed to give her speech on the stage, and Ms Rani looked at her angrily as she stumbled and stuttered. She caught her offstage and berated her about not being well prepared. Myra's heart sank even further. She looked around and saw a few suspicious glances thrown her way. No one seemed to be making eye contact, and even her usual companions seemed to give her a wide berth. She sighed as she left the assembly hall and went back to her empty classroom. She just wanted the whole thing to go away.

'Oh why, oh why did I pick this stupid topic?' she cursed herself. 'I should have done something boring like the Cold War or something.'

She had never spoken to Sreedevi in all her months in this new school, and that girl had ripped into her like an angry bear. She ached physically from the verbal assault. And it looked like her friends wouldn't be coming anywhere near her now. Even Noorie had disappeared after a while. Myra picked up her bag and got into the school bus parked below in the courtyard. She couldn't wait to get home and away from this mess. She wanted to lay her head on her mother's warm lap and cry her eyes out. And she was terrified about going back to school the next day.

Noorie sat quietly while Sreedevi's words raged around her. Sreedevi was in a terrible mood. The boarders of class 7 had grouped together for a talk about the latest problem. They stood in the back compound, near the old green winding staircase. Frankly speaking, Noorie couldn't understand what the fuss was all about. Why was Sreedevi getting worked up about something that happened so long ago? She wasn't even born then, was she? Fine, so they had been on opposite sides of the issue, but she felt that Sreedevi had ripped into Myra with needless violence. She could have voiced her opinions without so much malice. She believed Myra was Indian but she decided to keep quiet about her opinions. She didn't want to speak up and get into trouble herself.

Noorie watched the faces of the other girls as they listened to Sreedevi giving them a short history lesson about Kashmir and its long-standing issues. Savita was looking at her with such adoration that Noorie felt sick. She spotted Arthi listening with one ear to what Sreedevi was saying, while watching the nearby volleyball game.

One could see she wasn't really interested in the whole mess. Usha was watching Sreedevi with her sneaky eyes and she was nodding vigorously in agreement.

'So, girls, I think we should boycott Myra,' announced Sreedevi. 'We won't talk to her or play with her or anything. It will be like she doesn't exist, OK?'

Usha, Meenu, and few others agreed openly while others like Radhica, Jenna, and Arthi just shuffled their feet and looked here and there. They were still undecided. Sreedevi turned to face Noorie.

'And you? What about you? Are you with us or her? We know you are her friend,' she said scornfully.

Noorie didn't like being in the position she was right now. She had never liked tough choices. In her opinion, you always regretted it one way or the other. She knew what they were all thinking. Would she stick up for a day scholar yet again? Or would she stick with the boarders?

'I'm with you,' she said, but she noticed that her chest tightened and a weird lump had settled in her throat.

'*You are throwing your friend under the bus!*' her conscience cried out at her.

*How can you do this? She is your friend! She helped you. She stood by you when these very same girls boycotted you a few weeks ago. How can you forget that? And has she done anything wrong? She can't help the family she was born into, can she? And she is just as Indian as you are!*

Noorie shook her head to get the accusing voice out of her ears but to no avail. Her conscience plagued her for the rest of the evening, and she tossed and turned in bed, worried about Myra and what the next day would bring.

# Chapter 15

# TRAITOR

The big white letters slapped her in the face as Myra entered the classroom the next day. Someone had written the words on the blackboard and on her wooden desk. It had taken her every ounce of courage in her body to make her way to the classroom that morning. But that one word was enough to make her resolve crumble and destroy her confidence. There were hushed whispers in the classroom and Myra kept her head down. She didn't want anyone to see the tears swimming in her eyes.

Noorie walked in late along with Arthi. They had been hunting for Arthi's maths classwork notebook that was missing that morning. The minute they walked into class, the girls knew something was not right. The atmosphere was heavy with poison.

'Shit! Look at that!' whispered Arthi, nudging Noorie as they took their seats.

Noorie read the word and immediately turned back to look at Myra but she was looking down. She tried to make out if she was crying but all she could see was the parting of her hair. She was vigorously cleaning the top of the wooden desk with her handkerchief.

'This is horrible,' she whispered back.

'You think Sreedevi did this?' asked Arthi.

'Who else?'

'Do we rub it out? I don't think it's the right thing . . . to call her a traitor, I mean,' mumbled Noorie.

Arthi looked at her curiously and Noorie looked away. She was trying to understand what was going on in Noorie's mind just then. *Was she changing her view? Didn't she say she was with the boarders yesterday? Was she having second thoughts?*

*'Well, I don't think what they are saying is right and I don't think Myra has done anything wrong. She is who she is and there is no need to apologize for that,'* thought Arthi.

She looked again at Noorie, who was pretending to be busy with her books. She knew her friend had a kind heart but not often a strong spine. And she also understood that Noorie wanted to stand by Myra but was afraid to do so. *But hadn't Myra helped her when she was going through a bad time? Maybe it was her turn to be the Good Samaritan now.*

'Listen, I don't think this is right. They can't do this to her. I'm going to rub it out. And I'm going to complain about it to Ms Rani. Are you with me?' asked Arthi.

Noorie looked up and saw the steel in Arthi's eyes. She wanted to hug her friend and thank her for her strength and compassion. She wished she had her guts and spirit. She nodded and squeezed Arthi's hand.

Arthi stood up and walked over to the blackboard. The classroom went silent and every eye in the room was fixed on Arthi.

'This is wrong! This thing you are doing is *wrong!*' she yelled, taking the white duster in hand.

She turned around and started rubbing the board with vigorous strokes. The large white letters had almost filled up the entire blackboard, and it took Arthi a few minutes to clean it. No one said a word while she worked. Myra was watching with a poker face. She didn't know whether to be happy or sad that she was creating a rift in the class.

The class erupted in boos and sneers. Sreedevi walked over to Arthi and they were in a middle of a heated argument when Ms Jalu walked in. The class fell silent immediately and the girls quickly took their places. The first lesson that day was Ms Rani's but it looked like Ms Jalu was substituting for her.

'Good morning, girls,' she said, looking around curiously. 'What was all the noise about?'

No one said a word. Ms Jalu continued to look around sternly. She was a senior teacher with years of experience under her belt. She had moved to Ooty from Bombay years ago after marrying her husband, who was a local Ooty man.

'What? Cat got your tongue? I want to know what the ruckus was all about,' she asked, her voice rising slowly.

Ms Jalu was the kind of teacher even the seniors were scared of. No one messed with her lessons. They turned up to her class on time, paid attention during the lessons, did their homework, and submitted their assignments on time. Ms Jalu was a tough cookie and the juniors were warned in advance about her.

Arthi was in a dilemma. She didn't know whether to bring it up here or with Ms Rani. She looked at Noorie through the corner of her eye and saw her shake her head slightly indicating *no*.

'You! You, girl! Stand up! Why are your eyes and nose red? Were you crying?' Ms Jalu pounced on Myra. The others jumped in their seats.

'No, no, ma'am. I just have a c-cold. That's all,' stuttered a terrified Myra.

'You juniors and your antics. I don't have time for this. Turn to chapter 6 in your textbook. We will learn something new today.' She dismissed the issue and moved on quickly.

The class gave a silent but collective sigh of relief. Sreedevi looked at Myra strangely. *Why hadn't she said anything to Ms Jalu?*

The rest of the class avoided Myra like the plague, during break time. Arthi and Noorie walked over to her desk, where she was munching some glucose biscuits.

'Thanks . . . thanks for doing that,' mumbled Myra with a faint smile. She looked dazed like someone had hit her with a brick.

Arthi just shrugged; she never knew how to take compliments.

'We should speak to someone. One of the teachers, maybe? This is not healthy for the class,' said Noorie, her forehead creased with worry.

'Yes, but who? Ms Rani?' asked Arthi.

'Did you tell your parents?' asked Noorie suddenly.

'No! I don't want them to worry. And if I tell my dad, then the first thing he will do is walk into Sr. Rosemary's office. I don't want to get anyone into trouble. It will just get worse for me,' said Myra, looking scared.

Arthi and Noorie got several dark looks when they went for lunch. Sreedevi cornered Noorie near the study hall and spoke to her.

'What do you think you are doing? I thought you were done with all that day-scholar crap!'

'It's not that! Look, she is being targeted not because she is a *day scholar* but because she doesn't *seem* Indian enough,' replied Noorie.

'I don't think you should get involved in this. Why should it bother you so much? You and Arthi both!'

'Because we are her friends. And we can't just abandon her.'

'So then, yesterday? Why did you agree to side with us then?' asked an angry Sreedevi.

'I was confused, OK? And a little scared. But now I'm sure about what I'm doing,' said Noorie in a rising voice.

'I don't get it. Anyway, I just wanted to warn you. Watch your back now!' she said ominously.

Sreedevi walked away, leaving a shaken Noorie behind. She cursed her weakness and wished she were spunky like Arthi. All through the day, she was plagued by dark thoughts and she kept playing various scenarios in her head, all of which ended badly.

Noorie was getting ready for bed in the Yellow Dorm after a tense dinner. Arthi was in the bathroom and so she was alone. She was so lost in her thoughts that she barely noticed Jenna approaching her bed.

'Is it because you are a Muslim? Is that why you are sympathetic?' Jenna asked softly.

Noorie had been startled. She hadn't even thought of it that way. *Of course she knew she was a Muslim, but her religion had never coloured her thoughts or opinions before. Or for that matter, her friendships.*

'Of course not! It's not that! I am her *friend*. Then how do you explain what Arthi is doing? It has *nothing* to do with religion,' she said firmly. Jenna looked at her quizzically for a few seconds as if trying to make sense of it all but failing to do so. She just shook her head and walked away quietly.

Noorie took Arthi aside and told her about her conversations with Sreedevi and Jenna.

'It may get a little ugly. So we better be careful,' warned Arthi.

'Are you sure we mustn't speak to any of the teachers?' asked Noorie, looking fearful.

'It will die down in a few days. Just stop focusing so much on it,' snapped Arthi. She was getting tired of her friend's timidity.

Noorie lay in bed mulling over Jenna's words. *Religion had never been brought up before, ever!* She thought about all the friends she had had earlier and now; she had *never* thought about their religious beliefs. All she had looked for when she sought friends was whether they were on the same wavelength or not. For that matter, while her parents were devout Muslims, they had so many friends who were Christians and Hindus. In Kerala, religion was never a cause for a divide. She thought about the dinner-table conversations at home where her father and uncle discussed plans for Onam and Christmas with equal gusto as they did for Eid.

Every festival was a cause for celebration irrespective of the religious beliefs behind it. They laid out beautiful flower-carpets for Onam just like their neighbours did. She remembered sitting shoulder to shoulder with her friends on the floor, sampling the many goodies that were laid out on the green banana leaf as was the Kerala tradition for Onam. There had been no *Muslim-Hindu* business, they had always come together as one, as *Malayalees. But today a simple question about her religion had shaken her. Why?* She couldn't understand why she was so perturbed. Her worries seeped into her soft pillow as she laid her head down for a much needed rest. She hoped things would get better as Arthi predicted.

But it didn't get any better. It got worse. The next day, no one talked to either Arthi or Noorie. They were ostracized and it became very lonely for them. No one played with them or sat near them by choice. The entire class ignored them, and the girls' morale dipped lower and lower as the week moved ahead. To make things worse, someone began playing nasty pranks on them. Their notebooks went missing. Someone tore out Noorie's completed homework from her maths book; that got her into trouble with Ms Sindhu. Arthi's science project was smeared with ink and she had to redo the whole chart. Noorie was sent out of class during English because she couldn't find her English textbook in her bag and she could have sworn she had packed it that morning. They found spiders under their pillow and dead cockroaches in their study hall desks, and all they could do was hold on to each other for support and pray it would end soon.

'How much longer can we endure this?' asked Noorie one evening after more than a week of hostility.

The day before, someone had thrown down her bag and stepped on all her books while she was at PE class. She stared at the muddy footprints on her English textbook and felt the tears rolling down. Arthi was at her wits' end too.

'Let's go to Ms Rani,' relented Arthi.

They waited outside the staff room during lunch break the next day. Usha saw them and she hurried to inform Sreedevi. She had been the one who had played all the nasty tricks on the two girls. She enjoyed these things—pouring ink, tearing pages, hiding books, etc. In fact she was really enjoying herself this past week. Noorie's and Arthi's expressions of dismay and horror only made her hug herself with glee. Too bad she couldn't get her hands on that Myra's books, else she would have done something creative there too.

Ms Rani took the girls into a corner in the library and heard their story. She had known her class was not the way it had been at the beginning of the term, but she hadn't been able to decipher the problem. The more she heard, the more concerned she became. Such strong words and actions could inflict permanent trauma on young children. She realized she had to resolve the matter immediately, before things got out of hand. She decided to discuss the matter with someone more experienced than her: Ms Jalu.

Sreedevi, Savita, and Usha sat on one side of the polished oak table in the conference room, while Arthi, Noorie, and Myra sat on the other side. The six girls were pointedly ignoring each other as they waited for the adults to join them. Sreedevi and her gang had been displeased when they were called for the mediation.

'Snitches,' they had whispered in the Yellow Dorm the previous night. But Arthi and Noorie refused to be baited into an argument.

Ms Jalu entered the room and the girls jumped to their feet. She looked severe with her hair tied back and her large eyes bulged even more. Ms Rani and two senior girls followed her. Sreedevi gasped when she saw them. They were her cousins Janaki and Mridula. *Why were they here?* She tried to catch their eye but they ignored her.

'Now, girls, I have been given an idea of what has happened but I would like to hear it again, from the horse's mouth. So let's start with Myra,' she said, gesturing to her.

Myra took a deep breath and looked at Arthi and Noorie, who nodded, urging her to speak up. She started hesitantly. She was a peaceful child and she had never been in a situation like this before where she had to voice her thoughts and anguish, especially before the very people who perpetrated those acts against her. But she knew this matter had to be put to rest and this was her chance to do so. As she spoke, her confidence increased. Noorie had never heard her friend voice her thoughts and fears before, and her heart seized when she heard her cry. She thanked her lucky stars for her family, friends, and neighbours and most of all, for being born in a secular state like Kerala, where it didn't matter where you were from! Arthi was listening intently too, her eyes bright with unshed tears and her fists clenched. Ms Jalu's lips tightened into a straight line and her gaze became sterner.

Sreedevi was stubborn though. 'Ma'am, I'm not trying to say anything wrong. Myra's family is from Muzaffarabad, which is in Pakistan-occupied Kashmir. It is under Pakistan control and so that makes her a Pakistani. She has no right to call herself an Indian, at least not in my view.'

Ms Jalu looked at her for a moment but didn't comment.

Instead she asked, 'Now who has been playing all these pranks on Noorie and Arthi?'

Usha squirmed a little in her chair while both Sreedevi and Savita looked clueless. Noorie and Arthi were surprised. They had believed it was Sreedevi who had perpetrated all the attacks against them.

'I think I have my answer right here,' said Ms Jalu, nodding towards Usha. 'I'll send you to Sr. Rosemary to get what's due for you, Usha.'

Usha blanched in fear at the thought of meeting the principal. She didn't say anything but kept her head down.

'Now,' continued Ms Jalu, looking at everybody, 'listen carefully to what I have to say. The Kashmir problem is something that has been simmering for decades. People have very different views about it, and I'm not here to justify one or the other. We are all entitled to have our opinions and our beliefs; in fact we encourage freethinking and nurture a spirit of enquiry in this school. Ours is a country where we have people belonging to different religions and cultures but we have found a way to live together in reasonable harmony. Of course, there will always be troublemakers who try to exploit weaknesses here and there and try to convert everything into a communal issue. We absolutely do not encourage such behaviour here.'

Ms Jalu paused and looked specifically at Sreedevi and Myra before continuing.

'The freedom fighters and leaders of our great nation must have had some sense of what they were doing when they decided to have two separate nations, India and Pakistan. But remember, before independence we were one and the same. As you grow older and see more of the world, you will realize that we are probably more similar to our neighbours than we believed. These problems you see in newspapers, they are always perpetrated by a handful of people. Most of them are illiterate or have something to gain politically or financially. As children, you must always keep an open mind. Don't become rigid and narrow-minded. Myra has stated her case quite eloquently, she has told us what she and her family believe in and *that's* what makes her who she is. It is our *individual* values and beliefs that define our personality, our identity, not just something our *great-grandfathers* did. Do you understand?'

Sreedevi's face had lost its arrogance and she had been listening carefully to Ms Jalu. She nodded slightly. One of Sreedevi's cousins, Janaki, spoke up.

'Sree, even in Kashmir it is only a small minority of people who are always stirring up trouble. The majority of the people want to just lead peaceful lives. Our family has friends across all religions and we even have close friends in POK. Our views may be different but we have agreed to disagree, you see? After all, a few decades ago we were all the same till these lines were drawn on the map to separate us. Myra would be culturally closer to us than any of our other friends from the South. Her family has the same connection to our land as we do. Let's not label people and stereotype them. You remember the conversations we have at home, your papa and mine? They always speak for peace and harmony, and they want the same progress and prosperity across all classes of society. These wars have hurt our family and we have lost many relatives but so has Myra. Her family gave up their home and came here to make a life. She is more *like* us than *unlike*. Our grandmother's social work does not discriminate. She embraces everyone and treats them all equally, and that is the example she would expect us to follow as well.'

Mridula spoke up: 'Sreedevi, at the end of the day, we are all Kashmiris, be it Hindu or Muslim. We are bonded together by the fact that we speak one language—*Koshur*. We are all ethnic Kashmiris and we may live in different parts of India or Pakistan or anywhere else in the world but there so many things like culture, traditions, and customs that we share, across religions and even across borders. Myra is as Kashmiri as we are. She is as Indian as we are!'

The room was quiet as Mridula's words rang out. Noorie and Arthi listened to her with rising admiration. It all made perfect sense to Noorie. What she had said was absolutely right. Back home in Kerala, it was language that bound them all together irrespective of religion, caste, or creed.

She remembered her father's words: 'We all have the same roots. Many years ago some of our ancestors converted into Christianity and Islam while some of us stayed on as Hindus. So at the end of the day we are all the same, we are all Indian.'

Myra's eyes were moist. Finally, someone was able to understand her situation and put it across in the right way. She caught Mridula's eye at the end and smiled gratefully. For a few minutes, no one said anything.

'I'm . . . I'm sorry. I spoke out of turn,' mumbled Sreedevi numbly. She was caught up in a rush of emotions. She had an image of her stately grandmother, who didn't look very pleased at Sreedevi. Her shoulders slumped as she realized she had let her emotions run wild and had let her family down. They had always spoken of peace and compromise and here she was doing the opposite. She groaned inwardly and kicked herself for her foolishness. Her grandmother's charity was working to help all people, she didn't discriminate, and she had seen so much more of life than Sreedevi had. Sreedevi felt foolish and very, very petty.

'Myra, I'm really sorry. I shouldn't have . . . shouldn't have . . .' she stuttered, looking at Myra.

'It's all right. I'm just happy you understand,' said Myra with a radiant smile.

'And you too . . . I'm sorry,' said Sreedevi, nodding at Noorie and Arthi.

Everyone in the room was smiling except Usha. She had been hoping for a showdown and now it looked like everyone was going to be best friends again.

'What terrible luck! And now *I'm* the one who is going to the principal! How unfair!' she thought. She looked malevolently at Noorie, Arthi, and Myra.

'I'll make them pay,' she thought, 'somehow!'

# Chapter 16

# WINTER IS COMING

U sha decided to miss morning studies on Sunday. She had been scheming all night. Thankfully it was bright and sunny though a bitterly cold wind blew. Winter was almost upon them and the days were getting shorter and colder. The girls spent more time in the study hall or playroom than outside in the chill. She walked briskly across the empty back compound that looked so sad without the usual laughing children. She heard the bell for morning studies ringing in the distance, and she hoped she wouldn't be missed. But then again, she didn't really have any friends who cared so much that they would be worried if she went missing. That stupid Meenu she hung out with wouldn't even notice she was gone; she would be balancing chemistry equations just for fun instead. Usha hated that she didn't have any real friends. It had always been like this, even in her old school. She made an effort but no one seemed to like her. Her elder sister Ilai was popular though and that made it hurt more.

'Why can't you be more like Ilai?' her mother always asked, and it broke Usha's heart every time she said it.

Usha walked briskly and reached the duck pond in the farm faster than she expected and thankfully she hadn't met anyone. The trees shielded the pond from prying eyes. Usha knew of the pond's existence from her elder sister. Last month, they had had a science class at this very spot. Their biology teacher had arranged it and Ilai had spoken about the pretty pond at length. They had been learning about metamorphosis and the teacher wanted to show the children frogs and tadpoles in their natural habitat. Apparently the pond had plenty of them, and her sister and her classmates had caught a slimy green frog just for fun but had to let it go because their teacher had been horrified.

Usha looked at the mirror-like surface of the near-circular pond. There were no ducks to ruin the calm and Usha sat down on a nearby rock and to admire it. She couldn't hear any frogs croaking and she wondered if she would have to abort her plan. *There would be no plan if there was no frog*, she thought. She walked around the pond. Ilai had told her that they had found their frog between some of the rocks that lay at the muddy side of the pond. Usha's sports shoes made a squelching sound as she stepped into the gooey mud near the water. *It's not as pretty as it looks*, thought Usha with disgust. She hated getting dirty, and as she looked down, she down she noticed that her brand-new Nikes were covered with orange-brown mud. She gave an exasperated sigh. All this would be for nothing if she didn't find a nasty-looking frog!

But the gods smiled upon her after almost twenty minutes of hunting, and she found a massive, ugly toad with disgusting warts all over its greenish-black skin.

'Noorie is going to love this one!' thought Usha as she managed to catch it and place it in an old shoebox with holes. Her fingers felt slimy after touching the toad, and she almost gagged when she smelt her fingertips.

'Ugh! Disgusting!' she muttered as she washed her hands quickly in the pond.

Usha planned to keep the toad in her study hall locker and grinned when she heard a loud croak.

'Hey! You there! What are you doing here?' someone shouted from between the trees.

Usha turned to find Sr. Elizabeth peering at her from her below her large straw hat.

'Who is that? You aren't allowed here!' Sr. Elizabeth yelled angrily as she walked swiftly towards Usha.

She stood frozen for a moment but then realized she would be in a big mess if she were caught and so she turned and ran.

'Stop! Stop!' shouted Sr. Elizabeth.

But Usha ran like the wind, hugging her shoebox tightly. She didn't even turn around to see if Sr. Elizabeth was following her; she just ran like the devil was after her.

'Hey, Noorie. Can you clean the blackboard and teacher's table for me tomorrow morning? I have to meet Ms Sindhu for some help with my maths lesson,' said Radhica.

As class leader, Radhica had the responsibility to make sure the blackboard was clean, the chalk box filled, and the teacher's table kept tidy before each class.

'Sure. I can do that for you. I'll just do it before morning studies. Don't worry!' replied Noorie, pleased she was asked to do this. Things were on the mend with the rest of her classmates. At least Radhica and Jenna were behaving normally. Sreedevi and Savita were polite but avoided both her and Arthi but she guessed it was because they were embarrassed and nothing else.

Usha listened to the conversation with glee. Her plan just got an upgrade. She would use the toad not on Noorie or Arthi but on the teacher. She giggled and hugged herself. Meenu, who was beside her, looked at her strangely and then moved away. Usha didn't even notice. She was too busy making changes to her plan. She had to find a way to place the toad in the teacher's desk without anyone catching her, and she had to time it after Noorie finished tidying up; that way she could pin it on Noorie.

The first lesson on Monday morning was science, and Usha hoped Ms Bartley would insist that Noorie be expelled or suspended or something equally brutal once she was caught as the culprit. Usha had skipped morning studies and had followed Noorie and slipped in the toad just after she had left the classroom. None of the day scholars had arrived yet and so Usha was in luck. She was in and out of the class like a ghost.

Ms Anita walked into the class 7 classroom red-faced with exhaustion. She took science for the junior classes and she was just waiting to go for her maternity leave. She was eight months pregnant and her belly was already quite huge. Ms Bartley had called in sick that morning and so she had to cover her class even though it was her last day. She had been looking forward to a quiet morning, sipping warm tea in the staff room and here she was saddled with a class she had never taught before. The girls were staring at her belly and she was beginning to feel irritated already.

'Good morning, girls. Have a seat, please! Can someone bring me the textbook?' she asked. She sat gingerly in the straight-backed wooden chair; her back just hurt all the time.

Radhica ran up with her textbook and she took out the lesson they were currently on. Ms Anita nodded and dismissed her with a wave of her hand and she had a look at the chapter in question.

'Ma'am, you have to take attendance. It's the first lesson,' reminded Radhica.

'Ah! OK. Where's the attendance register?' asked Ms Anita.

'In the teacher's table, ma'am,' she replied.

Usha held her breath as Ms Anita opened the teacher's table. She hoped Toadie would do his part. For a moment, nothing happened and then all at once Ms Anita's screams rent the air. The whole class was startled.

'Ahhh! Aaaaah! Fff-rog! Get it off me! Get it offfff! *Aaah*!' screeched Ms Anita.

An ugly greenish-black blob sat on her stiff upper arm and gave a loud croak. The girls were both stunned and fascinated. Usha laughed silently at everyone's expressions. *This was so much fun! Why hadn't she thought of things like this before?*

'Get it offfff!' Ms Anita screamed like a maniac. She had stood up now and was trying to throw off the stubborn toad. She screamed shrilly for a few more seconds and then suddenly she crumpled in a large heap onto the floor. The girls gasped in panic; they had never seen a teacher faint before.

Myra sprang forward, yelling, 'Help me! Someone please call the school nurse!'

She took Ms Anita's head in her arms and saw that she was unconscious and unhurt. She thought of what her father had taught her. The other girls were crowding around, worried.

'Don't crowd! Please clear the space. She needs to breathe,' said Myra, taking charge.

'Listen to her,' yelled Radhica, 'Move back!'

'Try waking her up!'

'Here! Put some water on her face!'

'Oh no! Is she dead?'

'Shut up!'

'Oh, shit!'

'Where is that frickin' frog?'

The class was in an uproar and the girls were so caught up with the happenings that they didn't notice Sr. Rosemary enter the classroom. She had been taking a lesson for class 8 next door and she had heard the yells and had come to investigate. The air in the room became a few degrees cooler with her entry, and the girls turned around to find her staring at them trying to take stock of the situation.

'Class leader! What is going on here?' she exclaimed in mounting alarm as she found the heavily pregnant teacher unconscious on the floor, with her head in Myra's lap.

Before Radhica could explain, Noorie ran in with school nurse, and the next few minutes were spent reviving Ms Anita and calling for an ambulance. The class waited silently for the ambulance to arrive. Ms Anita sat up groggily and was embarrassed to find the principal in the room. Sr. Rosemary took Radhica aside to get a blow-by-blow account of the events of the morning. Her expression became grim, and her lips were pulled into a straight line by the end of the conversation.

Myra's father rushed in with the nurses; he had come personally to see to Ms Anita. He nodded at Myra with a smile when he heard what she had done. He squeezed her shoulder, and Myra glowed with pleasure.

Radhica and Noorie stood in the principal's office. Sr. Rosemary was pacing in her office, trying to find the culprit.

'Did you place the frog there, Noorie?' she asked for the hundredth time.

'No! No, Sister. I swear I didn't! I promise!' cried Noorie.

All evidence pointed towards her. Radhica had washed her hands of it by saying Noorie was the one who cleaned the desk that morning.

'Did you know Ms Anita was coming today? Do you know she has high blood pressure and she could have died? You could have killed her and her child!' said Sr. Rosemary quietly.

She was able to make Noorie's knees tremble without even raising her voice. Her fury was cold and silent.

'Sister, it's not me! I . . . I . . .' And Noorie broke down.

'I don't want your tears! I want the truth!' said Sr. Rosemary, shaking her head angrily. 'I'll have to write home to your parents, do you realize that? We don't encourage nasty pranks like this.'

Someone knocked on the door, and all three of them turned to see who it was. Sr. Elizabeth stood there in her crisp white habit but she still wore her Wellingtons (scrubbed clean) and her enormous straw hat.

'Yes, Sister?' muttered Sr. Rosemary, looking irritated. Her moustache quivered.

'I'm sorry to disturb you, Sister, but I have actually come to complain about one of your girls,' she said.

Sr. Rosemary sighed and her shoulders slumped for a moment. Her problems seemed endless.

'What now?' she asked, raising her invisible eyebrows.

'I caught one of the girls near the duck pond on Sunday. I tried to stop her but she ran away. I want you to announce in assembly that the farm, duck pond, woods, and orchards are off-bounds for the students. I don't want children getting lost or worse,' insisted Sr. Elizabeth, her face creased with worry.

'Sure, sure!' said Sr. Rosemary, dismissing her concerns. She had bigger problems at hand now.

'So, you will announce it?' persisted the nun.

'Yes! Yes, I will, Sister,' sighed Sr. Rosemary.

Sr. Elizabeth didn't seem very satisfied but she decided to leave the matter for now. Perhaps she could talk to the boarding mistress as well, she thought as she made her way to the door. She left in a huff.

Sr. Rosemary was quiet for a few moments.

'Where did you find the toad?' she asked Noorie with a queer look on her face.

'I . . . I didn't find it, Sister,' sobbed Noorie. 'I'm terrified of them.'

'No! No . . . if you had to find a frog, where would you go?' she asked suddenly.

'The duck pond, I guess?' replied Radhica without thinking.

She remembered something her older sister had told her, about some bio class near the pond.

Sr. Rosemary stared at the two girls without speaking for a few seconds.

'Radhica! Run out and find Sr. Elizabeth! Bring her back here right away!'

Radhica was surprised; she didn't get it but she ran out anyway.

Sr. Elizabeth had just turned the corner at the end of the long corridor, but Radhica had caught a glimpse of her hat.

'Sister! Sister!' she yelled and ran. The corridor was empty as all the students were in class. Her voice rang out but Sr. Elizabeth didn't seem to hear her.

She ran and the corridor echoed with the sound of her black shoes hitting the flat grey stone tiles. She caught up with Sr. Elizabeth just as she entered the convent garden. She took a few seconds to catch her breath but then explained why she was there and both Sr. Elizabeth and Radhica half walked, half ran to the principal's office.

'Sister, please come with me!' said Sr. Rosemary leading the way to class 7.

'What's going on?' asked Radhica.

Noorie shrugged. She had no idea where Sr. Rosemary was going with all this. The girls followed the two nuns back to their classroom. Ms Sindhu was in the middle of explaining compound interest to a bug-eyed class of girls.

'Please excuse us, Ms Sindhu,' said Sr. Rosemary.

'Oh? Why, certainly, Sister,' said Ms Sindhu, looking a little flustered. It wasn't every day that the principal ran into your classroom.

Usha had been busy doodling in her rough book and was hardly paying attention until the intrusion. She turned white when she saw Sr. Elizabeth standing behind Sr. Rosemary.

'Oh-oh! This can't be good!' she exclaimed mentally. She tried to hide behind the head of the girl in front of her but unfortunately she was much shorter than Usha and afforded minimal cover.

'Sister, if you would be so kind as to take a look at the girls in this classroom. Do you think any of them could be one of the girls you saw on Sunday?' she asked invitingly.

Sr. Elizabeth was quite pleased with the principal's extremely prompt response to her complaint. This was unusual for Sr. Rosemary, who usually turned a deaf ear to most of her issues. Sr. Elizabeth stepped forward, eager to recognize the troublemaker and impress Sr. Rosemary with her superior observation skills.

'Oh dear! In their uniforms they all look the same!' she thought with mounting dismay. She was walking between the rows now and peering into the faces of the girls. There were a few giggles at her comical antics but they quickly became hushed as Sr. Rosemary cleared her throat sternly.

Usha was in the back of the class. She tried to screw up her face and looked into her maths textbook with increasing concentration.

'Can you look up, dear? I can't quite see your face,' said Sr. Elizabeth softly.

Usha knew her time was up. She sighed and looked up at Sr. Elizabeth. The nun peered into her face and her mouth became an 'O' as she recognized the girl from the duck pond. She turned to Sr. Rosemary and nodded towards Usha.

'Come along now. We have something to talk about,' said Sr. Rosemary, gesturing for Usha to come forward. The class burst into agitated conversation as soon the two nuns left, and Ms Sindhu gave up trying to explain compound interest; there were only ten minutes left of the lesson any way.

'Wow! I mean, wow!' exclaimed Priya at the dining table at dinner that night.

'Even I couldn't have thought about something like that!'

'You're impressed by what Usha did?' snapped Arthi. 'She almost killed Ms Anita and got Noorie into trouble.'

'Oh, gosh! Stop being so melodramatic! I'm just saying the prank was a good one. I'm not saying her motive was good, OK?' replied Priya.

The girls were discussing the events of the day and they were talking in whispers, for Usha was sitting at the nearby table, drinking soup. She looked ill with worry. No one knew what had happened in Sr. Rosemary's office but they guessed it had to be bad for Usha.

'Serves her right!' hissed Radhica. 'She gave us all a bad name. God! I hope Ms Anita is okay. We have to speak to Myra about her tomorrow.'

'I'm just glad it's over!' said Noorie, smiling with relief. She thought she would go grey with worry when the whole thing had put her in the spotlight.

'And about time too! Exams start in two weeks and we have a truckload to study,' said Jenna. 'I feel sick just thinking about it.'

The girls groaned and moved on to the next topic of discussion. Exam week was headed their way and no one had started revising; that is, no one except Meenu, of course!

# Chapter 17

# HOLIDAYS

'Put down your pens, girls! Stop writing immediately. Your two hours are up!' said the invigilator in Noorie's classroom. For the past week, these three sentences had evoked a sharp panic in her, and her hands had shivered as she tied the exam papers together after each exam. But today she had been waiting for it. It meant the term was over and that they were finally free to go home. *Home! Oh! She couldn't wait to see her parents.*

She met Arthi and Myra in the corridor outside the classroom. The girls were in different classrooms for the exam week. They had been shuffled and their seating had been all over the school.

'I can't believe it! We survived the first term!' exclaimed Arthi.

Myra laughed and clapped her back. She was happy for her friends. They would be going home today after six months. She wondered what it was like, being a boarder, away from her parents and her dadu. *It must be so hard for them to be away from all whom they love,* she thought.

'Look! Cars have already started to come!' said Arthi, hanging over the balcony railings.

'Careful! You don't want to fall off!' laughed Noorie. She spotted a shiny Mercedes near the trees. Sreedevi's car! She watched as her grandmother got out and made her way to the boarding mistress's office. *Oh! That woman could put a queen to shame with her grace!*

'Who's that my dad is talking to?' asked Myra suddenly.

Noorie hadn't noticed a man walking up to Sreedevi's grandmother. *Oh dear! It was Myra's father and he was talking to her. Oh! How she wished she could hear their conversation.*

'Ummm . . . that's Sreedevi's grandmother,' said Arthi hesitantly.

Myra started running towards the boarding mistress's office. Noorie and Arthi jogged along behind her, worried about what was happening. *Would it start up all over again?* By the time they ran around the horseshoe-shaped corridor to the other end, Sreedevi and her cousins had also joined the adults.

Noorie and Arthi were startled to find them all laughing.

'Myra! I was just talking about you!' said her father, surprised to find his daughter by his side suddenly.

'Madam! This is my daughter Myra! She is in the same class as your granddaughter, I believe!' he said innocently.

The other girls held their breaths. The older woman looked at Myra with interest.

'Another beautiful Kashmiri gem!' she said softly in Koshur, taking Myra's hand.

Myra smiled shyly and shook her hand.

'I am always so pleased when I find someone from home!' she said to Myra in their native tongue. 'And you, Doctor! You must visit us some time! It was such a pleasure meeting you and speaking Koshur so far away from home!' laughed the imperial woman.

The girls walked back to their classroom. They had to empty their desks before they left for the holidays. They noticed a crowd of people near the principal's office.

'What do you think's going on there?' asked Arthi.

'No clue! Any idea what's the deal with Usha?' asked Noorie.

The others shrugged. No one seemed to know what had transpired in the principal's office two weeks ago. Usha had returned looking chastised and had avoided all of them.

'Let's go and ask Ms Poornima,' said Myra suddenly.

'What, the secretary? As if she will tell you anything!' scoffed Arthi.

Myra looked at her as if trying to say 'watch and learn' and skipped over to the secretary.

'Hello, Ms Poornima! How are you?' She smiled sweetly.

'Oh! Hello, dear! I'm fine. I'm fine. How wouldn't I be? You father is my physician, no?' she gushed.

Myra looked over her shoulder and made a face at Arthi in jest.

'What's going on here? Why is there such a crowd?' she whispered conspiratorially.

'Oh! They are new admissions! For next term!' said Ms Poornima, looking through a blue file with a list of names.

'Oh? Any in our class?' asked Myra surprised.

'Tsk tsk. I'm not supposed to say anything.' Ms Poornima winked. 'But I'll give you a clue. There are three new girls joining you next term.'

'Three? Wow! Which ones?' asked Myra, pushing her luck.

'Off with you now!' said Ms Poornima, shooing them away with her blue file.

The girls were out of the lobby and in the corridor again. It was getting colder and they pulled their sweaters closer.

'Three new girls!' groaned Arthi.

'What? Why does it matter?' asked Noorie.

'Now we have to learn a whole new cast of characters just when we have made sense of who we already have in our class!' explained Arthi, exasperated.

'Oh, come on! Don't be a pessimist. It might be fun. We may have some interesting ones,' laughed Myra.

'Yeah! Like that one there,' said Arthi, pointing to a chubby girl with her hand inside an enormous packet of crisps.

'Wow! What is she eating? Can you read the name on the cover?' said Myra.

The girls squinted and tried to read the name on the red-and-blue cover.

'I think it says Oman Chips!' said Noorie triumphantly.

'Oman? Isn't that somewhere near Saudi Arabia?' asked Arthi.

'Yup!' said Noorie, who knew her geography.

'Interesting,' said Myra, looking at the girl chomping on the chips. She burped loud enough for them to hear and they giggled.

'Look! Look! There's a Chinese girl!' whispered Arthi excitedly.

They saw girl with oriental features step out of the principal's office, with her parents.

'But her mom is wearing a sari, silly! So she can't be Chinese!' observed Noorie.

'Ah!' said Arthi, slapping her forehead.

'Maybe her dad is Chinese and her mom Indian,' giggled Myra.

'No! They all *look* like Chinese but that doesn't mean they are! They could be from one of the north-eastern states,' pronounced Noorie.

The other two girls looked at her curiously like she had begun speaking Latin or Greek.

Noorie sighed in exasperation and explained that the people of the states in North-East India had oriental features and hence this girl could possibly be from Nagaland or Sikkim or Meghalaya or one of the others.

'Wow! Noorie, you are turning into Meenu!' teased Arthi.

'No! I'm not!' said Noorie hotly though she was secretly pleased she knew the answers where her friends didn't.

'So we found two of them! I wonder who the third one is,' mused Myra, tapping her chin.

'Girls! Girls! My car is here! My parents are here!' yelled Noorie suddenly as she spotted her father parking the car in the courtyard. Arthi and Myra watched as their friend ran like an Olympian weaving through the crowds. They laughed when she launched herself like a missile into her father's open arms. Myra watched Arthi's tender expression.

'Do you miss him?' she asked.

'What?' asked Arthi, startled.

'Your father. Do you miss him?' Myra asked again.

Arthi was quiet for a few seconds and Myra kicked herself mentally. Clearly this was a sore topic. Arthi continued to watched Noorie and her father. He held her by her shoulders and asked her something, to which she replied and threw her head back, laughing. She then stepped forward and hugged him tightly, and something broke inside Arthi.

'No! I don't miss *him*,' she said hoarsely. 'But I miss *that*!'

She could almost feel the warmth of their father-daughter embrace and she wished she could have it too. Myra took Arthi's hand and squeezed it gently. They stood silently side by side and waited for the sun to set on yet another cool Ooty evening.

3 1237 00354 3924

CPSIA information can be obtained
at www.ICGtesting.com
Printed in the USA
FFOW02n1948231017
41457FF